SILVER BLOOD, SHADOWED SKY

AMATERINA

Silver Blood, Shadowed Sky

By: Amaterina

Cover design by: Amaterina with assistance from CoPilot AI.

Printed in the United States of America

ISBN Digital: 979-8-9996931-2-9

ISBN Paperback: 979-8-9996931-3-6

Imprint: Independently published

You Reached Me

It wasn't easy
I didn't want to let you in
I had walls dressed in logic, overthinking
doors guarded by silence and previous hurt.

But you never forced your way in...
You just kept showing up,
giving me your quiet arms full of presence,
eyes that didn't show pity, only understanding
and love... and didn't flinch away from me.

And when I finally decided to open up,
just a small crack in the door -
you didn't rush in - didn't push.
You just stood there, waiting patiently,
gently, with love and understanding...
as if I was worth every moment -
no matter how long it took

You saw me, and you waited.

Amaterina

Prologue

The Legend of Selene

Before the packs. Before the bloodlines. Before the howl first touched the moon…
There was only chaos.

The werewolves roamed wild and separate, led by alphas who ruled through might, not merit. They waged war over land, blood, and pride, tearing through forests and kin with teeth soaked in the rage of the unchecked - taking what they wanted through their strength alone, never caring who suffered in their path.

The moon goddess, Selene, watched them from her silver throne above, her light bathing the earth in sorrow. She had shaped the wolves in wildness, but not in cruelty. Her heart ached to see them tear one another apart, ruthlessly. So, in the age before memory, she came down in secret—walking among them not as a goddess, but as one of their own. Searching, for one she deemed worthy. One who could change the tide of cruelty…

She found him beneath an ash tree, bleeding but not broken. Clinging to life with a strong will and heart that surpassed all she had found before.

An alpha who led not with power, but with purpose. His name was Joseph, and in his eyes, she saw balance. Justice. Kindness. Strength. Restraint. In him, Selene placed her faith. And for a time, her love.

To him, she bore twins under a harvest moon.

A son, born first – eyes gold as sunlit meadows, with a voice that calmed storms. He would inherit his father's spirit and be blessed with the ability to lead all wolves, not just his own pack — a true Alpha of Alphas. The strength and heart of his father would forever flow through his bloodline.

And a daughter, born second – wrapped in silence and silver light, her tiny hand glowing faintly with moonfire. In her flowed a sliver of Selene herself... power that would change form with each generation born, always reflecting a piece of the goddess's will. The blessings passed through her would bring prosperity, vision, and guidance to the wolves... a divine reminder of how they were meant to live.

But the peace was not to last. Selene could not remain among mortals forever, and her departure left a void. Jealous alphas rose again, fearful of the blessed children. Some sought to claim them. Others to end their bloodline.

So, in the age before memory, the family vanished into shadow—protected, hidden, and slowly divided by fate.

Yet not all was lost.

The son's line endured. Bearing the strength and leadership of both Alpha and Goddess. With each generation, a single heir was born to carry his power: the ability to lead all wolves, to command loyalty not just through might, but through legacy. These descendants eventually rose to rule as Alpha Kings. Guardians of balance, order, and strength.

The daughter's line, however, was different... Rarer.

Her blood carried a fragment of the Goddess herself – powerful. Unpredictable and ever-changing. Not every generation bore her gift, and when it surfaced, it did so in daughters marked by moonlight. One at a time. Always alone. Their presence was whispered of, never proven. Their stories became prophecy.

Twins were never born again. The gifts had split. One line to rule. One line to awaken. And only when balance tipped would the Moon's child return. Yet the prophecy endured.

"When the moon returns too soon,

And the wolf is born before her time,

When balance is broken,

and one is lost beneath the stars -

The child of the moon shall rise.

Marked by silver, shadow, and sorrow.

Cast out... yet destined to unite.

Her howl will summon truth.

Her heart will forge peace.

She must walk the path of flame and frost,

To awaken the old blood and face the veil.

Or else the packs shall fall to ruin."

It is said she will be known by the mark upon her wolf — A crescent moon at the center of her chest. And in her eyes, the memory of the goddess herself.

Chapter 1 - The Wolf Awakens

Selina sat cross-legged at the edge of the glade, where the tall grass swayed like whispers in the wind and golden sunlight streamed through the trees in narrow shafts. The air was crisp with the scent of damp earth, honeysuckle, and early summer... her favorite kind of morning. It should have felt peaceful. It usually did.

But today, everything felt... wrong. The scents and scene weren't bringing her the calm they have in the past.

Her head throbbed in slow, pulsing waves, as if something inside her was knocking... begging... to get out. It had started before dawn, dragging her from a tangled dream of silver eyes, shadowed trees... dark forests. Her temples burned, her chest ached, and her skin felt tight - too small for the bones underneath.

She had told no one. Of course not.

Not her father... he barely looked at her anymore, unless it was to remind her how she'd taken the life of the one person he loved. Not Denise, his chosen mate, who had barely spoken two words to her since moving in last year. She would rather sigh in disapproval. And certainly not Jennifer, her stepsister, who would have laughed, called her a freak or broken, then probably told the whole pack she was contagious.

Not even Luke.

Her older brother tried, in his quiet way. He'd slipped into her room that morning before the house stirred, brushing her hair gently behind her ear and placed a roll of sweetbread into her hand. "Happy birthday, Lina," he had whispered. "Stay out of the house today if you can. You know how Father gets." Then he kissed her forehead and disappeared again, dressed in his Beta trainee gear.

Slipping out of the house to go to the Alpha's house and the training that awaited him.

He was always gone lately. Training, duties, silence. Training came first now. The pack came first.

And she… She came last. Like always…

That was the way of things in her life – sweet moments followed by silence. Hints of love swallowed up by cold. Safety that never lasted long.

She curled her toes into the damp grass, grounding herself in the textures of the clearing trying to focus on the now. The glade was one of the few places that felt like hers. Hidden behind a line of moss-covered stones at the far edge of pack lands, it was nestled between thick trees and gnarled roots, forgotten by most. She liked it that way. No one came here, so she could claim it for herself.

Birdsong laced the treetops above, and a squirrel rustled along a nearby branch, flicking its tail. Sunlight glinted across the leaves like shards of gold. She should have felt safe here. But the ache inside her had only grown sharper.

She tried to breathe through the pain, slow and deep, like Luke had taught her.

In. One. Two. Three. Out. One. Two. Three.

But it didn't help. The pain didn't settle.

Because it wasn't just in her head anymore. It had sunk into her chest. Into her spine. Into her arms, fingers, and ribs, like something inside her had grown too big to stay hidden. Like she was splitting from the inside out. Expanding…

And then… everything stilled.

The squirrel froze. The wind suddenly stopped moving. Even the birds' morning melodies *fell* silent.

And she heard it.

"Selina."

The voice wasn't a whisper, not exactly. It echoed inside her mind and wrapped around her like silk—gentle and strange, ancient and intimate.

She jerked upright, clutched her arms, eyes darting around the clearing. "Who...?"

"Do not fear, little one. You will understand soon. This is all natural. I only wish I had more time to explain. I'm sorry."

The pain in her chest surged. Hot, sharp, sudden. A spike of pain radiating outward like lightning, stealing the air from her lungs. She collapsed onto her hands and knees, gasping for breath.

"I am Amaris," the voice said. Closer now. Clearer. *"I am you... and not you."*

Her vision blurred. Light shimmered at the edges of her sight, distorting the glade around her. The pressure inside her exploded into white-hot heat. Her bones ached as if they were being stretched, reshaped... pulled tight like a bowstring ready to snap.

And snap it did.

The first pop of her shoulder wrenched a scream from her throat, raw, abrupt, sharp. A crow startled into flight above, its wings beating a frantic rhythm into the air. Her scream twisted mid-breath... warped into a sound not human.

A growl.

Her fingers curled inward, shrinking, darkening. Fur sprouted along her arms, thick and black as ink. Her skin split and healed all at once, muscles shifting beneath the surface. Reshaping itself into something other, something wild. She wasn't breaking.

She was becoming.

Her knees gave out. Her spine arched backward. She hit the ground on all fours, panting, the world tilting sideways beneath her. Muscles trembling under the force of change.

She was shifting!?!

She wasn't supposed to be able to shift yet. They said it only happened at fourteen. This shouldn't be possible yet...

And her birthday had only just begun...

"We are early," the voice – Amaris – whispered again. *"You are waking before your time. You must not let them see. Not yet."*

And then Selina was no longer screaming, or falling, or afraid.

She was running.

Her feet... no, paws – thundered across the forest floor with impossible speed tearing through ferns and leaves. The wind whipped against her muzzle. Her lungs burned. Her senses... sharper than ever... opened wide.

She could smell everything: wild mushrooms, moss and pine bark, rabbit fur, and the metallic tang of running water. She could hear the heartbeat of the forest... The squirrels, the crows, even the breeze shifting overhead. Every crackle of leaf and whisper of branch was a new thread in the tapestry of sound.

And beneath it all, she felt Amaris.

Not just a voice now, but a presence. Calm. Steady. Protective. Fierce. Patient... Loving. She pulsed in Selina's blood, curled in her bones like moonlight given form.

"You are not broken, Selina," Amaris said softly. *"You are chosen."*

She darted around trees with ease, her new body moving like it had always belonged to her. Selina leapt over a fallen log and skidded to a stop beside the creek. The surface shimmered in the sunlight.

She looked down.

Two golden eyes stared back. Her fur was deep black, her ears tall and elegant. Her reflection shifted slightly... and there, in the center of her chest, glowing like moonlight through mist...

A white crescent moon. Right over her heart.

She blinked. The mark pulsed once. Then, as if sensing her thoughts, it faded slowly into her fur, still there, but hidden.

She sat back on her haunches, heart pounding in her chest. The reflection staring back at her, foreign and familiar – golden-eyed, sleek, wild. Powerful. The girl she had been was still in there peeking out, but now she shared her skin with something more.

What was happening to her? What would happen if the pack found out?

"You must hide me," Amaris said softly, gently. *"We are not ready. And they are not ready for us."*

"I don't understand," Selina whispered aloud, her voice strange on her lupine tongue. Breathy, low, and primal.

"You will understand. In time," Amaris said.

Selina turned from the water and padded slowly back through the trees, her body humming with new strength. The forest still thrummed with life, but it no longer overwhelmed her. Her body moved with silent confidence, every step purposeful, fluid. She could feel the strength in her limbs, the way her senses stretched out like invisible threads reaching for everything in the forest.

And when the shift began to reverse, this time slower, steadier, more controlled… she didn't resist. She trusted it. Her body shrank, fur receding, bones realigning with a faint crackle and pull. When it was over, she lay in the grass once more. Naked, damp with sweat, her muscles trembling, her skin slick and raw…. she found herself curled in the grass, her body aching but whole.

Her shredded clothes lay in pieces around where she initially shifted. She gathered what fabric she could and wrapped it around herself with shaking hands, then sat up with knees drawn to her chest, breath shallow and sharp. Her fingers felt longer, her vision sharper, breath deeper, hearing sharper. Her entire body buzzed, as if charged by moonlight itself.

Everything was changed. Her body. Her soul. Her place in the world. She had crossed a line and could never go back.

But where will that place be?

In the quiet that followed, she didn't feel empty. For the first time in her life, she didn't feel helpless.

But she had never felt more alone.

"You are the first," Amaris whispered one last time, her voice soft but sure. *"You are the warning. You are the beginning."*

Chapter 2 - Pack of Pain

Age 10 – One Week After the Shift

Selina sat at the edge of the school courtyard, hugging her knees to her chest. The gravel beneath her jeans pressed sharply into her skin, but she didn't move. If she stayed still enough, sometimes people forgot she was there.

A shadow fell across her.

"Hey, freak. Why are you hiding back here?"

She looked up just in time for a snowball to slam into her face. The ice stung, the cold biting deep into the raw skin of her cheek.

Three boys stood in a half-circle around her – sons of warriors, their postures oozing confidence, cruelty, and arrogance. The tallest one sneered.

"You lost?" he said, stepping closer. "Or did your imaginary wolf get scared and run away again?"

"She probably doesn't even have a scent," another muttered. "Bet she's human."

Selina opened her mouth to speak, but shut it again. Her heart thudded beneath her ribs like a trapped bird. Her wolf stirred uneasily, and with it came the familiar hush in her mind... Amaris's quiet, watchful presence.

"Let them," Amaris murmured. *"Let them believe what they want. We are safer this way."*

But It didn't feel safe. It felt like drowning.

One of the boys grabbed her braid and yanked hard, jerking her forward, almost causing her to hit her head on her bent knees.

"Maybe she just needs someone to wake it up," he taunted.

Selina bit the inside of her cheek until she tasted blood. She refused to cry. Not I front of them. *Never* in front of them...

When they finally left... laughing and shoving each other like it was just a game... she stayed there in the gravel. Long after the sting had faded. Long after the blood dried. The sting of their words biting more than their hands.

"You are not weak," Amaris said softly. *"You are simply not ready."*

*****

Age 11 – Late Spring

Selina limped behind the schoolhouse, clutching her elbow with one hand and wiping her bleeding lip with the other. Her shirt sleeve was torn where it had caught the flagpole during her fall – or rather, her "fall." The skin beneath throbbed, and her ribs ached from where she had hit the ground too hard. She ducked around the side of the building out of sight, and leaned back against the stone wall. Her breaths came shallow and uneven. She didn't cry. Wouldn't cry. Refused to cry. Not for them. She just needed a second.

Footsteps crunched in the grass.

"What happened?" Luke's voice was low and sharp with alarm. He crouched beside her, the Beta trainee insignia gleaming faintly on his shoulder in the late morning light. His eyes scanned her face and arms. Each bruise seemed to darken his expression further.

"I fell," Selina muttered.

"You always fall these days," he said tightly. "You were never this clumsy before." Selina noted his voice carried something brittle... frustration maybe? Or guilt?

She didn't meet his eyes.

"Jennifer tripped you again, didn't she?"

"I didn't say that."

"You didn't have to." He exhaled hard through his nose. "You have to start telling someone. This can't keep happening."

"No one listens." Her voice was barely more than a whisper. *No one cares anyway even if I told.*

Luke's expression cracked. Just a little... for a heartbeat she could see the guilt. He pulled off his jacket and gently draped it over her shoulders, careful not to touch the sore spots.

"They're wrong about you," he murmured, brushing a strand of hair from her cheek. "One day they'll see it."

Selina turned her head away, staring at the line of trees just beyond the schoolyard fence. She didn't answer.

She didn't believe him.

Not yet.

******

Age 11½ – Summer Lessons

The classroom reeked of damp stone and wet fur. Pack pups sat cross-legged on woven mats, fidgeting as Elder Maelin paced the front of the room. The lesson was on shifting etiquette... what to do, how to prepare, how to act when your wolf surfaced at age fourteen.

Selina sat quietly at the back, her hands clenched tight in her lap.

"And remember," Maelin was saying, "wolves that fail to shift by their fourteenth birthday are... well, unusual. Sometimes it means the wolf was never there to begin with. Sometimes it means they're too weak to hear the call."

A few snickers rippled through the room.

"She already looks human enough," someone muttered behind her. "Maybe she was born broken."

Selina felt her throat tighten. She didn't turn around.

Maelin's eyes fell on her. "Selina," she said, her voice cool and clipped. "I trust you're preparing for the day? Or... is there no point?"

Heat rushed to her face. The other pups turned toward her. Jennifer smirked from the front row.

"I'm preparing," Selina whispered. A lie. A necessary one to keep her secret... to continue to hide the truth.

Maelin didn't reply. She moved on as if Selina hadn't spoken at all.

******

Age 12 – First Full Moon of Autumn

The training yard stank of sweat, blood, and churned-up dirt. Selina knelt in the grass, scraping dried blood off the sparring mats with a dull brush. Her arms ached. Her hands were raw. No one offered to help.

Jennifer stood nearby, arms folded as she watched. "You want to be part of the pack so badly," she said sweetly, "you should act useful."

Selina didn't respond. She'd long since learned that silence was safer than defiance.

"Make sure you scrub under the weapons rack," one of the older boys said as he passed. "Don't want the wolfless trash leaving stains where the real wolves train."

Laughter rippled behind him.

Selina kept her head down and scraped harder, the bristles catching on a deep gouge in the wood. Her knuckles split open. Blood welled, fresh and red.

"I could end this," Amaris growled in a protective whisper. *"You need only ask."*

"I can't," Selina whispered. "Not yet. You said we had to wait, that it was too soon."

Amaris hesitated. Then: *"Yes. And I still believe that. But even I am learning... how heavy silence can be."*

*****

Age 13 – Midwinter

She sat on the frozen ground behind the house, her legs shaking, a damp towel pressed tightly to her ribs. The banister in the entryway had cracked beneath her when she'd "fallen" after Jennifer's elbow "accidentally" sent her flying down the stairs.

A splinter the size of a twig had pierced her side before she hit the floor. Now, it throbbed, angry and red beneath the towel.

The cold seeped into her skin, but she barely noticed. Numbness had a way of creeping in long before the frost.

Footsteps crunched over the brittle grass, fast and heavy. Then Luke dropped to his knees beside her, his face a storm of fury and panic…. She was pale. Silent. Barely moving. Barely breathing.

"Lina… What the hell…?"

He reached out, peeled back the towel gently, flinching at the blood-soaked edge and the deep bruise blooming over her ribs. His jaw clenched.

"She said it was an accident," Selina murmured.

"She's lying," he snapped. His voice was roughened, his wolf momentarily surfacing. "You should've told me!"

He wasn't there. Not when the bruises bloomed. Not when the silence burned louder than words. Finally, Selina whispered. "You weren't here. You're never here when the *accidents* happen." The words fell from her lips before she could soften them, and they hit him harder than she expected.

Luke recoiled slightly, pain flickering in his expression. "I'm trying," he said hoarsely. "I can't be everywhere, especially with the pack demands on my time."

"I know." Selina's voice was quiet but steady. She looked down at her bruises… shadows painted across her skin like ugly truths no one wanted to acknowledge. The puncture wound from the splinter had stopped bleeding, but it would scar. Another mark she'd have to hide.

"You have your place," she said after a long pause. Then she met his gaze evenly, her voice devoid of anger. Calm. Still. "And I have mine. You can't change that. Not when Father reinforces it with every look, every silence. And encourages it with the few comments he chooses to pass my way."

Luke looked away, shaking his head. "You don't deserve this."

"But I get it anyway," she whispered.

He knelt there, helpless. Guilt radiated off him like heat, but guilt didn't heal bones. It didn't erase bruises. It didn't change anything.

And for the first time, Amaris stirred... not as a whisper, but as a tremor. A restless, simmering presence.

"Let me teach them fear," she growled, low and dark. *"Just once."*

Selina leaned her head against the wall, closing her eyes, warring with her conscience, with what she knew she *should* do against what she felt she they *deserved*...

"Not yet," she said.

A pause.

"Then promise me this," Amaris said, voice tight with restraint. *"When the time comes, don't hold me back."*

Selina didn't answer. But in her silence, a promise curled in the cold.

******

Age 13½ – The Pack Run

The full moon hung high in the sky, casting a pale light across the ridge where the pack had gathered. Dozens of wolves stood ready to shift, bodies tense, some stretching their limbs, eyes gleaming with anticipation. It was one of the rare pack traditions where even unshifted wolves were allowed to participate, if only at a distance. A symbolic run. A shared ritual. A pack.

Selina stood apart from the others, near the edge of the tree line. Still in human form, arms crossed tightly across her chest. Waiting for the run to start. Still watching. Always watching. Always waiting. The run hadn't started, but she already felt left behind.

She wrapped her arms tighter around herself as the first howls rang out. Long, low, haunting. The pack began to shift. Bones cracked. Fur burst through skin. Bodies reshaped into fluid, primal power.

She wasn't supposed to run, not really. But sometimes they let her walk the trail behind them, after the official start. Just far enough to say she'd participated. A courtesy. A kindness. *A leash*…

 But not tonight.

"Not safe for someone like you," Jennifer purred sweetly as she passed, her wolf already clawing at the surface. "You might get trampled."

Selina didn't respond. Her jaw clenched tight enough to ache. She bit her tongue, tasting blood, desperately trying not to speak.

A group of older boys snickered as they passed, one holding something behind his back. The moonlight glinted off his teeth as he grinned.

"Wait!" one boy called. "Let's help her keep up!"

He hurled it. Mud, thick and wet…splattering across her front. Another boy followed suit, flinging a clump of leaves and dirt at her legs. A third smeared pine sap across her back as he walked by, laughing.

By the time the rest had shifted and thundered into the woods, Selina stood alone. Muddy. Sticky. Unseen.

She wiped a smear from her cheek with a shaking hand. The forest was silent again, save for the distant pounding of paws against earth.

"They don't see you because they refuse to," Amaris said softly. Her voice was a balm and a blade. *"But they will."*

Selina looked toward the trail—moonlight glimmering along the dirt like silver veins. Then turned toward the opposite direction.

She would not chase them.

She would walk her own path.

Alone if she had to.

"Let it settle," Amaris whispered. *"Let them believe they've won. For now…"*

******

Age 14 – The Night Before Her Birthday

Selina stood barefoot in the glade, moonlight spilling silver over her skin like a blessing and a warning. The woods were quiet, the air crisp and clean. Rain had passed earlier in the day, and the leaves still glistened with lingering droplets, like the trees themselves wept in silence under the stars.

She inhaled slowly. The scent of damp moss, cedar, and distant pine wrapped around her, grounding her in the space that had always been hers. A space forgotten by the pack. Her sanctuary.

But even here, peace didn't come.

"Tomorrow, they will expect the shift," Amaris gently whispered.

"I won't," Selina answered. Her voice didn't shake.

"Good," came the response. *"We are not ready. And neither are they."*

Selina exhaled, watching her breath curl into the cold air like a ghost leaving her chest. Her fingers clenched at her sides as she remembered….

Jennifer had cut the straps of her backpack again earlier that day. The contents had scattered across the commons. Books, clothes, half a sandwich, broken pencils. Everyone had watched. No one had helped.

Not even Luke.

He had seen. Making eye contact, he had paused. And then he walked away…

"Do you hate him?" Amaris asked softly.

Selina swallowed hard. "No," she whispered. "But I don't need him anymore. He has to follow his own path, and that no longer walks with mine."

A long silence passed. Then Amaris murmured, *"You are changing. You are crossing the threshold. You are beginning your transition. You are becoming."*

Selina lifted her chin, her eyes locking on the glowing arc of the moon overhead. The light pooled in her eyes and caught in her hair, turning her into something ethereal. Half girl, half shadow.

"I'm done waiting for them to see me," she said. "They don't have to."

The words settled like a vow.

And she…
She came last.
Like always.
But not forever.

Chapter 3 - Secrets Buried

Galen hadn't set foot in the east wing of the house in nearly fourteen years... but the guilt had never left it.

Even now, the dust resisted his steps, curling up in faint spirals as his boots crossed the old hall. Every creak of the floorboard sounded louder than it should have, echoing against faded wallpaper and memories he'd spent over a decade trying to bury... trying to erase.

The birthing room was still boarded shut. The thick planks he'd nailed across the door all those years ago remained in place. Weathered now, but unbroken. A physical barrier. A grave marker. A penance. One he never intended to cross again.

But something had driven him here today. Some pull he couldn't name. On the eve of her birthday – the nightmare's anniversary – he could no longer stay away.

He reached for the edge of the wood and pried one board loose with a groan of splitting nails. The scent hit him first... not rot, not decay, but the soft ghost of dried herbs and old sweat, of lavender and blood.

The scent of loss.

He slipped inside and closed the door behind him.

The room was smaller than he remembered. Or maybe his guilt had just made it feel larger back then. The narrow cot still sat in the center, covered in old linens yellowed with time. A cracked bowl rested near the hearth, its contents long turned to dust. On the wall above the bed, a faded tapestry fluttered in the draft... A moon woven in silver thread.

Everything else was as it had been that night.

His knees bent before he meant them to, and he sank to the edge of the cot. The wood groaned beneath his weight. He didn't care.

It had been raining that night.

He remembered because the storm had masked her first scream. He'd woken late—too late. By the time he burst into the room, Lyana was already slick with sweat, her face pale, her breath ragged. The healer was barked orders. The midwife looked panicked, already elbow-deep in blood-soaked linens.

"The herbs," Lyana had rasped, gripping his hand so tightly his knuckles cracked. "The mix... The moonroot and ironbark—it needs to be burned before... Galen, please..."

But it hadn't been there. She'd hidden it. No one had known what she was talking about until it was too late. Not even him.

"I didn't understand," he whispered now, voice hoarse in the still room. "Why didn't you tell me?"

The labor had been fast. Brutal.

Twins, the midwife had realized too late. Faster than any other birth the midwife had said.

The boy came first... Small, barely breathing. Struggling. He gasped once. Twice. Then silence.

And Lyana...

Lyana hadn't even had the strength to cry. Her lips were bloodless. Her hands trembled. But she turned her head to Galen with dazed, panic-filled eyes, whispered the word *"protect,"* and then...

She was gone.

Just like that.

One moment burning with life.

The next...Cold.

Empty.... Gone.

The girl came after.

Still and strange. Not crying. Not gasping. Just *watching*. Her eyes too wide, too knowing, as if she'd seen the veil from both sides. Staring – unblinking. Covered in blood, her tiny fists clenched around strands of amniotic silk. Galen had thought she was gone too... Another breath not drawn, another loss layered over the first two.

But then...

She opened her mouth.

Not to wail... but to breathe.

Steady. Strong.

Then her eyes had locked on his.

Dark. Ancient. Knowing. Not like a newborn at all. That look had haunted him ever since. Like she *knew*.

Knew what had just happened. *Knew* what she had taken.

Knew what she would become.

Something stirred now in the silence. Soft. Electric. Just beneath the surface. At the edge of hearing. Not memory. Not ghost. Something else.

A presence.

Faint….but watching.

He'd buried the boy before dawn—wrapped in wolfskin, placed beneath the roots of the ash tree where no one would look. The ground had been so wet the mud nearly swallowed the bundle from his hands.

Only the midwife had known. And she had kept her word, sealing her lips beneath the weight of his grief and fury. *"The goddess's touch is not always gentle,"* she had whispered. *"Sometimes the light burns."*

He hadn't asked what she meant. He hadn't cared then. Not then. Not while cradling the ruins of a life he couldn't save. He'd lost the only person he ever loved.

And all that remained was one of the children who had taken her.

Selina.

He hadn't been cruel to her at first—not exactly.

Just distant. Cold. Silent.

But as the years passed, as she grew into her mother's eyes, the same hair… as her voice began to carry the same edge of wisdom, the same stillness, the same knowing….the silence turned sharp. His distance, bitter. Grief curdled into *blame*. Because she reminded him. Too much… of what he had lost. Of what he hadn't protected. Of what he *feared* she might become.

It was easier than facing the truth. Easier than acknowledging that she reminded him too much of what he'd failed to protect.

Now, sitting here in the long-dead quiet, something inside him shifted.

He had seen her bruises lately. Too many, too often. Jennifer's lies, Denise's sneers, the warriors' cruel jokes. He knew. He just... hadn't stopped them.

He'd let the pack treat her like a ghost because it suited his guilt. Let her carry the weight of shame because it meant he didn't have to look inward.

And yet... she kept standing. Kept walking. Kept surviving.

He had seen the faint glow at her throat once, only for a second—after she touched the silver pendant in her room. A shimmer, like starlight. Like moonfire.

And he had seen her heal. Too quickly. Cuts that faded before they should. Bruises that never quite matched the stories. He had seen. And he had ignored.

Because to acknowledge it would mean confronting the prophecy Lyana feared and hoped for.

When balance is broken... and one is lost beneath the stars...

Selina had been born early. Had her wolf been awakened too soon? Her twin had died at birth. She bore the mark... He remembered it, faint and glowing in the first hour, a white crescent over her tiny heart.

And he had hidden it. Hidden everything.

Galen's fingers closed around the silver moon pendant still in his pocket. Lyana's. He'd found it beneath Selina's bed last week. She'd been visiting the old keepsake chest again.

She was asking questions. Looking for roots. He could not tell her. He didn't know how to tell her the truth. Some truths even he didn't know...

What if she hated him?

What if she forgave him?

He rose slowly, knees stiff, breath catching in his throat. The room felt too small. The memories too sharp.

But he couldn't destroy them. Not anymore.

He placed the pendant on the edge of the cot and turned to leave. Changing his mind at the last moment, he snatched it back.

As he stepped into the hall, his shoulders sagged beneath a weight he'd carried too long.

> The child of the moon shall rise...
> Marked by silver, shadow, and sorrow...

If the prophecy was true... if Selina was the child of the moon... then everything he had done might yet lead to her ruin. Her downfall... Or her *rise*.

Her becoming.

He closed the door behind him.

And this time, he did not lock it. The truth behind the door would be found eventually, so there was no point. He had a feeling the truth was coming soon... He didn't know what Selina would become. But for the first time in years, he would be watching...

Without walls. Without excuses. This time, not from a distance. Not from afar. Not in silence. But truly there.

******

Later that night, long after the halls had gone still and the hearths dimmed, Galen stood outside Selina's room.

He didn't knock. Just rested his hand against the wood.

He hadn't come this close in years. Through the door, he could hear her breathing... Slow and steady, already asleep.

A dozen words tried to rise. He bit them back. What would he even say? Instead, he laid the silver moon pendant on the floor just outside the threshold. He hesitated, fingers brushing the edge once more before pulling away.

Then, like a ghost, he disappeared down the corridor. Not ready to face her yet.

But willing, at least, to try.

He didn't see the door crack open moments later.

Didn't see her hand reach out to pull the pendant close. Didn't see the way her fingers curled around it like it mattered.

Didn't see the tear she refused to let fall.

But it was a start.

Even if the rest would soon crumble.

Chapter 4 - False Dawn

The morning of Selina's fourteenth birthday dawned clear. Cruel.

Frost clung to the windowpanes like a warning, glittering like shattered glass in the pale sunlight. Her breath clouded in front of her as she sat on the edge of her narrow bed, tugging a frayed sweater over her head. The fabric itched at the base of her throat and stretched tight across her chest, but she didn't care. She'd outgrown it months ago. No one had offered her a new one, not surprising at all.

She'd needed bras for at least a year now, too. But like so many other things, that hadn't happened either.

Below her, the pack compound was already alive with noise. Laughter echoed off the stone walls. The scent of meat pies and honeycakes drifted up from the kitchens. The entire territory buzzed with excitement. It was Shifting Day.

For most.

Selina flexed her fingers. They trembled, not from fear, but from restraint. Beneath her skin, Amaris stirred restlessly, her presence like a phantom heartbeat.

"They will expect a show," her wolf said calmly. *"We must give them silence. We can't let them suspect anything."*

A knock jolted her.

The knock wasn't polite or patient. Just three sharp raps followed by Denise's voice, thin and clipped.

"Don't make us late."

Selina stood. No one waited for her in the hallway... Of course not. She followed the sound of footsteps downstairs, where her father stood in full Beta regalia, shoulders squared, expression carved from ice.

He didn't look at her. Didn't speak. Didn't acknowledge her at all... *Did she really expect anything different?*

Jennifer bounced at his side, golden hair tied back with a silver ribbon that shimmered in the firelight. "It's going to be so *interesting* today," she said sweetly, her head tilted in faux curiosity glancing at Selina. "Do you think it hurts more if your wolf never shows up at all? Like your soul just decides to skip you?"

"Enough," Denise said mildly, though the lack of reprimand in her tone made the words completely meaningless. "We should go."

They walked together in brittle silence toward the heart of the territory, snow crunching beneath their boots. Selina trailed behind by a few steps... like always. Like she was supposed to do.

The Shifting Circle lay just beyond the Great Hall, ringed in smooth stone and towering moonpines. The snow had been swept from the open center, revealing a wide ring of packed earth and ash – sacred ground where power would rise or wither. Braziers lined the perimeter, flames licking skyward as the packs gathered. Stepping near the clearing with the circle felt like walking into a storm of eyes.

Dozens. Hundreds. Warriors cloaked in leather and fur. Elders draped in heavy ceremonial robes. Mates with children perched on hips or running near them, whispering and pointing. Even the Alpha King's envoy stood at attention. They had come to witness the moon's chosen rise. This cycle's transition. The true wolves...

Each month, on the night of the full moon, the packs of the region gathered for the Shifting Ceremony... a sacred rite marking those who had turned fourteen since the last lunar fullness. The event rotated between designated power circles scattered across the territory. This month, it was their turn to host. The Alpha King moved from one to the next, his presence both a blessing and a warning. Always attending. Always watching... Maybe even searching?

Selina stood on the outer rim, arms drawn tightly around herself. She could feel the energy in the air... An invisible hum beneath the skin, sharp and expectant. The circle pulsed with ancient magic, and it ached in her bones to stand here again.

Luke stood with the other Beta trainees, dressed in black and steel, his expression unreadable. His gaze flicked to hers briefly, then away. His hands were behind his back. Formal. Distant. Barely acknowledging her.

On the high platform at the head of the circle, Alpha Bradley lifted his arms. His voice boomed with the weight of authority.

"Today, we celebrate the next generation of our kind," he declared. "Those born under the protection of the moon and now called to awaken their wolves. Strength, loyalty, purpose... These will define who among you is worthy of this gift."

The names began.

One pack at a time, one by one, the new fourteen-year-olds stepping into the ring were called by name. One by one, the air filled with the crack of bones and the scream of transformation.

Each one facing the platform with the Alphas, the Alpha King, and his entourage.

A boy from the Blackridge pack shifted with a howl that echoed through the trees. Later a girl from the Red Moon pack cried tears of joy as she stood in her wolf for the first time. Both of their parents had rushed forward to embrace them, cheers erupting from every side of the ring. Slowly, 22 teens from fifteen other packs took their turn in their circle. All of them transformed into various shades of wolves, receiving praise and cheers from their family, pack members and Alpha.

Selina remained still, her body taut with the effort of staying motionless.

Your time is near, Amaris whispered, calm despite the storm swirling within her. *Breathe slowly. Let them believe you are small.*

The last shifter from her pack bowed out to applause. Only one remained.

Then her name rang out like a slap in the cold air.

"Selina Raines."

The crowd hushed.

She stepped forward.

Each footfall on the frozen earth echoed louder than it should have, pressing into her ears like thunder. Eyes followed her... Curious, pitying, some cruel, some cold. She didn't look at them. She couldn't.

She stepped into the center of the ring, the sky wide and cold above her. Her sweater, too small and stretched across her chest, tugged with every breath. She crossed her arms reflexively, too late to miss the brief flicker in Xavier's gaze as it dropped downward for a fraction of a second, then snap back to her face, his jaw tightening. Nathaniel's arms folded across his chest, his mouth a hard line, though his eyes lingered a moment longer than they should have.

Across the circle, the Alpha's sons stood like carved stone. Xavier, sharp-jawed and unreadable. Nathaniel caught somewhere between curiosity and something darker. Not pity. Not cruelty. Something that looked like confusion. Frustration even. As if resenting the fact that he noticed her at all.

And beyond them stood Jennifer, all sugar and venom, her smile sharpened by anticipation. She was here for the spectacle. Waiting to watch her fail.

Selina closed her eyes, shutting out the stares, the cold, the ache in her ribs.

On the raised dais, the Alpha King leaned forward, his gaze narrowing.

Beneath her frayed sweater, something flickered... So faint it could've been imagined. A soft pulse of silver, just below her left collarbone, like moonlight glinting through fog.

The Alpha King's eyes sharpened. But the moment vanished before he could grasp it. No one else stirred. And she hadn't shifted. Not even a tremble.

A trick of the light, he told himself, though a strange unease coiled in his gut.

The energy of the circle climbed her spine, wrapping around her like invisible vines... ancient and insistent. The magic *wanted* her to shift. It *called* to her. She could feel the crescent moon on her chest pulse with the power of the circle.

She ignored it.

"Hold," Amaris, she breathed inwardly. *"Just hold."*

Pain bloomed in her ribs, deep and tight, as her wolf instinctively fought to rise.

The crowd waited. And waited.

Nothing happened.

The silence stretched too long. A murmur began.

"Is she even trying?"

"Bet her wolf never even existed."

"She always was strange…"

"Freak."

"She probably faked the signs."

"Maybe she's human."

Selina held her expression steady, though her jaw throbbed from how tightly she clenched it.

Amaris quieted beneath her skin like a fading ember. The pulsing in her moon slowing, then halting altogether.

And then, Alpha Bradley stepped forward.

"There is no wolf," he said, his voice flat. "She has not shifted. She will be marked as wolfless."

The Alpha King's brow furrowed ever so slightly. He said nothing. But he would be watching. And perhaps, her history needs a little quiet investigation…

Gasps and snickers rippled outward like ripples in a pond.

Luke shifted his stance, tension rippling across his shoulders. Nathaniel's brow furrowed just slightly. Xavier didn't move.

Jennifer beamed.

The Alpha's voice cut through it all. "From this day forward, she will not be permitted in future shift trainings or patrol paths. Her presence during pack runs will be considered a risk. She is to remain within inner pack boundaries unless otherwise ordered."

Selina's hands balled into fists.

There it was. Final. Public. A brand burned without fire.

She bowed her head… Not out of shame, but because the act of holding in the scream pressing up her throat took every ounce of strength she had. If only they knew…

Then she turned and walked out of the circle.

No one called after her. No one stopped her. No one comforted her.

They'd gotten what they wanted.

She was wolfless.

Invisible.

Nothing.

But as she stepped into the shadow of the trees, the pain finally unwound, replaced by something else… Something low and slow-burning.

They believe the lie, Amaris whispered. *You gave them exactly what they wanted.*

Selina looked down at her hand. The faintest flicker of silver danced at her fingertips. Sharp, defiant, and unseen beneath the fabric of her sleeve.

"I hope they choke on it," she whispered, low and steady.

*****

From the edge of the circle, Galen watched her go.

His fists were clenched so tightly, his knuckles had gone white. He hadn't spoken. Hadn't intervened.

He'd watched the judgment pass. Had stood there while his daughter was branded wolfless – worthless in their eyes.

It was easier that way. He told himself it was mercy. That it would be safer if she was ignored. That no one would come for her if no one thought she mattered.

But deep down, he knew it wasn't mercy. It was fear.

Because if she really was the girl from the prophecy… if the moon's mark still lived in her… Then today had just confirmed something far more dangerous:

She could lie to them. She could lie and they can't tell…

And she would.

He turned away before she vanished into the trees. He couldn't bear to watch her disappear.

Not again.

Chapter 5 - The Pack Ghost

By morning, Selina's name had become something else entirely.

Ghost.

It followed her through the halls like frostbite... Silent and sharp. Where once they whispered "runt" or "strange," now they muttered the new word with cruel delight. Their smirks hidden behind hands and half-lidded glances.

"The Pack Ghost," someone giggled as she passed the outer courtyard. "You know, because she's got no wolf. Just a shadow."

Selina kept walking. Head down. Shoulders hunched. Invisible was better. Expected. Safer.

She no longer ate in the main hall. Too many times, her tray had been knocked from her hands by "accident." Too many times, her seat had been mysteriously taken. So she waited until after the lunch bell faded and snuck into the kitchens through the back corridor, hoping there might be leftovers... Hard biscuits, wilted greens, cold meat scraped from the bone. Scraps.

Some days there was nothing.

She'd started skipping meals. Not out of choice, but necessity. Her stomach shrank. Her energy waned. But she endured it quietly. Enduring had become her best skill. Scraping by on just enough...

At home, silence had grown thick and moldy.

Denise no longer spoke to her unless to give an order. Chores stacked like punishment: scrub the floors, sort the laundry, clean the hearth, gather kindling… Even when the snow bit through her gloves. And always, Jennifer found new ways to needle her with fake sweetness.

"Oh, poor little ghost-girl," she said once, tossing a scarf into the fire when Selina reached for it. "So cold without a wolf, aren't you?"

Selina had said nothing.

She had grown used to curling up in the corner of her room at night, beneath the narrow windowsill where the shadows pooled. Her bed had become a target – its covers yanked off, its frame smeared with ink or glue or worse. The floor, at least, did not betray her.

In the dark, she would press her hands over her ribs, where the ache from holding back Amaris still lingered.

"I'm here," her wolf whispered, curled deep inside her like an ember.

"I know," Selina whispered back. "I'm trying."

"We both are. But they can't see yet. Not until the time is right."

She counted the cracks in the wooden floorboards. She traced the moon's arc through the frost-glazed window. And when she was alone, really alone, she let herself breathe fully. Let the flicker of power spark at her fingertips. Let the glow of the crescent under her skin return for just a breath.

A secret rebellion.

****

A week after the ceremony, Selina stood at the edge of the training fields, gathering up broken arrows and stray gear left behind by the warrior cadets. It was part of her new "duty," apparently. She'd been assigned to cleanup.

As she bent to collect a discarded spear, she heard them.

Two boys from the older ranks, muttering behind the weapons shed.

"I heard the Alpha King looked at her during the shift," one said. "Like he saw something."

"Maybe he did. Maybe she's cursed. Or a traitor. My uncle said sometimes witches can fake a wolf's scent. That's why her eyes are so dark."

"Or maybe she's just dead inside. I mean... they're calling her the Pack Ghost for a reason."

They laughed.

Selina stood, arrow gripped so tightly in her hand it snapped in two.

*****

That night, back in her corner, she lay awake listening to the wind howl through the cracks in the walls. Her stomach hurt. Her legs ached. Her chest felt heavy.

They hate me, she whispered.

"They fear what they don't understand," Amaris said. *"But their fear will turn to awe. One day. You just have to wait."*

"Promise?"

"I swear it."

Outside, the moon rose over the trees.

Inside, a silver pulse beat beneath her skin, soft and unseen.

****

Two weeks after the ceremony, Selina was ordered to help prepare the Great Hall for a private celebration… The joint birthday of the Alpha's sons and her brother Luke. All three had just turned sixteen.

She scrubbed floors and polished the long dining tables while warriors hung lanterns and decorations above her. The scent of roasted meat and sugared wine filled the air. Laughter drifted through the halls. She wasn't invited. Of course she wasn't.

As the guests began to arrive, she was sent to serve drinks and carry trays. She moved through the room like a shadow, eyes down, invisible among the laughter and dancing. Jennifer made sure she stayed busy, always directing her to the messiest spills and the heaviest trays.

From across the room, Selina caught the twins watching her.

Nathaniel's gaze narrowed whenever someone bumped into her too hard. Xavier's eyes lingered too long when she bent to collect broken glass. Neither spoke. Neither helped. But neither looked away.

Later, when the guests had thinned and her hands were raw from scrubbing, she caught Nathaniel murmuring to Luke at the edge of the hearth.

"She doesn't act like she's broken," he said quietly.

Luke's answer was barely audible. "She never has been."

Selina didn't let herself react. Not then.

But something in her chest shifted. She was no longer Selina Raines.

She was the girl without a wolf. The one they wouldn't see coming.

The Pack Ghost.

Chapter 6 – Shadows and Smoke

The snow melted slowly that spring, revealing muddy paths and brittle grass as the earth stirred back to life. Training resumed at full force for the seventeen-year-old warrior ranks, and with it came new and creative torments.

Selina was fifteen now. Taller. Leaner. Stronger.

A year had passed since the Shifting Ceremony, but her name still drifted through the air… like a whispered curse. Ghost. Wolfless. Other. The pack had long since stopped pretending they didn't see her… They saw her plenty…

When they wanted to sneer.

To shove. To spit.

What was once whispers, have turned to open mockery now. A chorus.

Not just *Ghost* anymore.

Witch.

 Cursed.

Dead Eyes.

She heard it in the halls. Saw it chalked on the walls. Felt it in the way people moved past her... Deliberately close, just to shoulder-check her or spill a drink, or to stay purposefully distant … as if she were contagious.

Each morning, she was ordered to report early to the sparring fields to clean the equipment and scrape the frost from the weapons and practice area before drills began. By the time the others arrived, her fingers were already numb, her sleeves soaked with dew.

No one spoke to her.

Except to sneer.

"Ghost," someone muttered as they passed. "Try not to curse the gear with your touch."

"Bet she watches us train and imagines she's one of us. Creepy."

"Careful," one boy muttered as she passed the edge of the training field. "Wouldn't want the ghost to steal your soul."

Another chimed in, laughing, "Too late. I think she already ate it."

Selina didn't flinch. Not anymore.

She walked with her head down. Spine straight Face carved from ice. The bruises on her arms were old. The ones on her ribs, newer. Her lips didn't move, but her fingers itched with hidden light.

She was learning.

Learning how to quiet her rage. Learning how to listen in silence. Learning how to survive. And hide… Always hide what she was.

Jennifer led the whispers now with an almost regal flair. At sixteen, she was all polish and perfection… to most. Golden hair coiled like a crown, lips painted berry-red, smiles sly as knives. Her venom was sweet as honey, voice syrup-thick, especially when a male was near.

She had made herself the darling of the junior ranks, holding court at the center of every circle. Her eyes rarely left the Alpha twins.

Selina noticed.

Everyone did.

Jennifer's laughter always rang louder when Nathaniel was near. Her touches lingered too long on Xavier's arm. Her stories swelled with more drama, exaggerated and artful, designed to draw attention. To highlight her. And the girls around her mirrored it. Fed off it. Drew blood with their words because their queen demanded it. And their favorite target… was always Selina.

"Careful," she warned two younger girls in the corridor one morning, her voice sugary and loud enough for Selina to hear. "If you look her in the eye too long, you might lose your wolf. Or your soul."

The girls giggled and scurried away.

Selina kept walking, fists clenched at her sides.

Later that week, she found her boots filled with mud and ice water. Her books were missing from the library shelf, replaced with ripped pages that fluttered like broken wings to the floor when she opened the covers. Her gloves were gone. Again.

Still, she said nothing.

Not when she was tripped. Not when she was mocked. Not even when Jennifer "*accidentally*" shoved her into a stone pillar hard enough to leave bruises along her ribs.

The bruises faded faster than they should have… Like always.

Jennifer was also ruthless in other ways...

"Oops," she cooed once, knocking over a full bucket of icy water just as Selina reached for it. "Clumsy me. Better clean that up, ghost-girl."

Selina said nothing. Bent. Cleaned.

The twins had grown taller. Stronger. Their shifts had matured into something dangerous... Fluid, fast, commanding. At seventeen now, it showed. Xavier had become broad-shouldered and silent as a glacier. Nathaniel sharper, quicker with his tongue, and colder with his temper.

Jennifer had noticed.

She spent her days orbiting them. Smiling. Flirting. Dropping hints. Her hair always perfectly braided. Her neck deliberately bare to show off the moon-shaped birthmark she claimed was "*a sign of fate.*"

Selina noticed too. She was always watching. Always cataloging every movement in silence. The way Xavier stiffened when Jennifer touched his arm. The way Nathaniel rolled his eyes behind her back.

And the way – every now and then – both of them would look at Selina like they didn't understand what they were seeing.

Like they *wanted* to.

Like they didn't *like* that they did.

****

"Isn't it sad?" Jennifer mused one morning as Selina scrubbed the corridor outside the girls' training hall. "No wolf. No strength. No future. Just... leftovers."

"Why hasn't she run off into the woods yet?" another girl asked.

"Probably too scared. Or maybe she likes being pathetic."

Selina didn't speak. But the bucket she carried sloshed over when her grip tightened.

Amaris hummed beneath her skin.

"Not yet," Selina whispered. *"Not yet."*

At lunch, she was made to serve the others. She moved silently between crowded benches, eyes down, tray steady. When she passed the twins—Xavier with his stoic jaw and unreadable gaze, Nathaniel with his sharp tongue and restless stance— she felt their attention shift, pausing in their conversations.

Their gazes tracked her.

Always watching.

Never meeting her gaze.

And somehow, that was worse. Because it meant they *did* see her. And still chose not to acknowledge her.

Except when they did.

Once, while refilling cups, she stepped forward and felt the sting of something sharp drive into her heel. Glass. Deliberately placed. The sting shot up her leg. She stumbled. Caught herself. Bit her lip... and said nothing.

Nathaniel's eyes snapped to the floor. Her foot. Then to the smear of blood she left behind. His brow furrowed. But he remained silent.

"She's bleeding," someone snorted nearby. "Guess ghosts aren't dead after all."

Selina knelt to clean it, dabbing the blood from the stone with the edge of her sleeve.

Xavier's jaw flexed. He didn't speak either. Neither of the twins laugh with everyone else.

*****

One afternoon, Selina was ordered to sweep the steps outside the Alpha's council chambers while the senior meetings took place inside. She moved mechanically... broom in hand, eyes lowered, her body on autopilot.

When the doors opened, voices spilled out like smoke. Her father was the first to emerge.

Beta Galen's face was carved from granite, unreadable as ever. He barely acknowledged her presence. Just a passing glance. Cold and fleeting. But his stride slowed for half a heartbeat. As if something caught in his chest. As if he wanted to speak, and couldn't.

Luke followed behind him.

Seventeen now. Taller, broader, dressed in the sharp dark lines of a Beta apprentice. He looked every inch the role he worked toward. Every inch the future his father approved of.

Until his gaze landed on her.

His jaw clenched. His hands curled into fists at his sides.

"You shouldn't be out here," he muttered under his breath, low enough for no one else to hear. "You should be training. Running."

"They said I'm not allowed," Selina answered softly.

Luke's mouth flattened into a thin, frustrated line. "That doesn't make it right."

Galen glanced back. Just once. "Finish your work," he said, voice clipped. Distant.

Selina bowed her head. "Yes, Beta."

But Luke didn't move. He lingered in the doorway, the weight of her words still heavy in the air…

"I'm sorry," he murmured, voice strained and quiet.

Then he followed their father into the courtyard, his shoulders rigid… his eyes burning at her truth.

*****

At the week's end, the training compound held its mid-season drills. The junior wolves took to the field, demonstrating their strength for the elders and elite warriors.

Selina, of course, wasn't on the roster. She was told to help clean.

She stood at the edge of the field, sweeping muddy snow into uneven piles while the others sparred under full sunlight.

On the raised platform, the Alpha twins stood watching.

Xavier leaned against the railing, arms crossed. Nathaniel stood beside him, expression unreadable, eyes scanning the activity below.

When Jennifer stepped onto the mat and flipped a rival with a clean, practiced sweep of the leg, applause followed. She preened under the attention, her smile wide and polished as she cast a look toward the platform.

Xavier didn't move or react.

But Nathaniel's gaze drifted. Past Jennifer. Past the crowd.

To Selina.

She looked up… just as he looked away.

Something pulsed at her fingertips. Not anger. Not power.

Recognition.

*****

During sparring matches on the training fields, Selina was often assigned to collect arrows or reset the targets. She did so without protest, her presence barely acknowledged, her silence expected.

Until the day Jennifer cornered her near the edge of the archery range, flanked by two girls from the hunter lines.

"You missed a target," Jennifer said sweetly, pointing toward one still stuck across the field. "Better go get it."

It was still mid-practice. Arrows were flying. Warriors were actively shooting.

"That's not safe," Selina replied quietly, her voice low but steady.

Jennifer's smile sharpened. "Then you should move faster."

A laugh rose behind them. Selina turned slightly... Nathaniel stood with the other trainees, bow lowered, jaw clenched.

He didn't speak.

Didn't interfere.

Xavier's eyes tracked the moment.

From the arrow. To Selina. Then Jennifer.

He didn't move either.

So Selina turned... and stepped into the field.

The moment she stepped forward, a shot whistled past her shoulder... too close. Another thudded into the dirt beside her foot.

She didn't flinch.

She walked across the range, plucked the arrow from the target, and turned with it griped in her hand.

Steady steps. No hesitation. She walked back with arrows raining down around her.

She handed it to Jennifer without a word.

For a moment, the field held its breath. No one moved.

Then Jennifer laughed and waved her off like she was nothing.

But Xavier was still watching.

And Nathaniel looked away… too quickly. Too guilty.

****

As the training ground cleared out and long shadows stretched across the field, Selina stayed behind to gather the scattered gear. A snapped arrow here. A discarded shield there. Leftovers. Forgotten pieces.

The sun had dipped below the trees when it happened.

A stray bolt – carelessly released – sliced through the air across the range. Fast. Silent. Deadly.

It was heading straight for Xavier.

He didn't see it.

Selina did.

Her body moved before thought could. She lunged, grabbed a cracked training shield from the pile and hurling it forward… in front of him… just in time.

The bolt slammed into the wood with a thud…

Inches from Xavier's chest… before crashing *into* his chest…

The shaft still vibrating where it impaled the shield.

Xavier spun around. "What the hell… ?"

She didn't answer. She bent to pick up the broken arrow, as if the danger hadn't bushed inches from his heart. As if saving him meant nothing.

His brows drew low. "That could've…. "

"It didn't," she said flatly, already turning away.

"How did you... ?"

Selina cut him off, her voice sharp. "It doesn't matter. *Ghost*, remember?" The she spun on her heel and stomped off.

Behind her, Nathaniel stood motionless at the edge of the range. He had seen everything. He hadn't moved. Was Unable to act before she did.

And he was still watching. Silent.

*****

That night, Selina sat in her usual corner in her room, legs curled beneath her, eyes half-lidded as shadows danced across the walls. The stars blinked beyond the frost-laced glass. Distant, indifferent, and eternal.

"*I saw you*," Amaris whispered. "*They saw you too*."

"Let them look," Selina murmured. "I won't bow."

"*You never have.*"

She was no longer the child they had tried to erase.

She was still "*wolfless*." Still alone.

But beneath her skin, the crescent moon glowed. Pulsed.

And she was done being afraid.

*****

The following week, she was told to deliver training gear to the storage barn... Alone. It was a half-mile from the main compound, and dusk was already bleeding into night.

The barn loomed like a shadow.

She pushed open the creaking door, arms full, and was immediately shoved from behind.

Jennifer. Of course.

With her came two other girls. Kara and Min – both snickering, both cruel.

"You're not supposed to be here," Jennifer said, eyes gleaming. "This is for wolves."

Selina said nothing.

They circled her.

"I bet you pretend," Kara whispered. "At night. That you're one of us. That someone *wants* you."

Min laughed. "Maybe she dreams about the twins. Thinks they'll save her."

Jennifer stepped closer. "Do you? Dream about them?" she purred. "Is that why you always *linger* when they're near?"

"I don't," Selina whispered.

A slap cracked across her cheek.

"You don't speak unless spoken to," Jennifer hissed.

Selina's head turned, but she stayed upright.

Amaris stirred. A low growl beneath her ribs.

Not yet, Selina told her.

Then a noise. Outside. Boots on gravel.

The girls froze.

A beat later, Xavier's voice cut through the air. "Leave her."

The others scattered like startled birds. Jennifer lingered, mouth twisted, but then she, too, vanished into the dark.

Selina didn't turn.

She didn't have to.

"I didn't ask for help," she said quietly.

"You didn't have to," Xavier replied. Then he walked away.

*****

That night, Selina curled against the wall in her narrow room, cheek stinging, hands trembling.

"They hate me," she murmured.

"*They don't understand you*," Amaris whispered.

Selina let a spark of power flicker at her fingertips.

"They will."

Chapter 7 – Marked and Cast

The morning of the Alpha twins' eighteenth birthday dawn clear and cold, the wind laced with frost and expectation. Celebration buzzed through the compound like wildfire – banners strung across stone walls, long tables piled with feasts, laughter already echoing from every corridor.

The pack had been preparing for weeks. Selina had been working twice as long to make it happen.

At dawn, she scrubbed the floors of the Great Hall, her fingers raw and stinging. She polished silver trays until her arms ached. She wasn't invited. Of course not.

But she was expected to serve. Expected to be invisible. Expected to smile.

"Make sure the table arrangements are perfect," Denise snapped, thrusting a bundle of linens at her. "And stay out of sight once the guests arrive. No one wants to see the pack ghost haunting their feast."

"Yes, ma'am," Selina replied, her voice flat and practiced.

Inside, the Great Hall had been transformed. Long tables glittered with crystal and firelight. Plates overflowed with roasted meat, honey-drizzled bread, and golden apples perfumed the air with their warmth and spice.

At the head of the room, two throne-like chairs had been placed – one for each twin.

Xavier and Nathaniel. Now of age. Now men. Warriors.

Future leaders. Future Alphas.

Selina caught only glimpses of them during the celebration.

Xavier stood near the hearth, calm and unreadable, surrounded by the elite trainees. Nathaniel laughed with a circle of warriors... but when his gaze swept the hall and landed on her working, his smile faltered.

She looked away.

She didn't see the way his jaw tightened.

Jennifer was radiant in a silver dress, her golden hair twisted into intricate braids and pinned with moonstone combs. She clung to Xavier's arm for most of the evening, though his hand remained still. Unmoved. Stiff.

She brought him drinks, whispered jokes, lingered far too close.

When Nathaniel walked past her to refill his plate, she looped her fingers around his wrist.

"You'll dance with me later, won't you?" she purred.

Nathaniel gave her a look—flat and unreadable. He nodded once.

Her eyes glinted with triumph. But they flicked, just once across the room. To Selina.

She had noticed the way the twins had started to glance Selina's way. Even when they didn't speak. Even when they didn't smile. Especially then.

And she hated it.

*****

Later that night, long after the Great Hall had emptied and the fires burned low, Xavier stood alone in the corridor outside the western balcony. His hands braced on the railing, eyes fixed on the dark horizon.

The chill bit at his skin, but it was nothing compared to the tension coiling in his chest.

"She's different," Nathaniel said from behind him, stepping out of the shadows. His voice was low.

Xavier didn't turn. "You feel it too."

Nathaniel nodded once, his jaw tight. "Since yesterday. Maybe longer. Every time she's near, something in me… " He exhaled, sharp and unsettled. "It doesn't make sense. She's wolfless."

"No," Xavier said quietly. "She's not."

Nathaniel's brows lifted, surprise flickering behind his cool gaze.

"There's power in her," Xavier continued. "I can feel it. Like static under my skin. And every time she looks at me… "

"You want to go to her," Nathaniel finished, barely above a whisper.

They stood in silence for a beat, the weight of truth sinking between them like stones dropped in still water.

"She's ours," Xavier said at last, his voice low and rough with certainty. "But she doesn't know. Not yet."

Nathaniel nodded slowly. "And we can't claim her until she does."

"Not without breaking the laws," Xavier added.

"And not without tearing the pack in half."

A sudden click of heels echoed down the stone corridor.

Jennifer. They both quietly growled.

Her voice followed a moment later... sweet and syruped. "There you two are. I've been looking everywhere."

Xavier's face closed off instantly, his expression going flat. Nathaniel turned as well, the emotional weight between them locked away behind practiced walls.

Jennifer tilted her head, all faux concern. "Everything alright?"

"We're fine," Xavier said, voice cool and unreadable.

She narrowed her eyes slightly, sensing something charged in the air but unable to name it. "You looked... serious."

Nathaniel offered a tight smile... all surface. "Just discussing tomorrow's drills."

"Of course." She looped her arm through Xavier's without asking. "Come. You can walk me to my quarters."

He didn't protest. But his posture remained tense, his jaw tight.

But as they disappeared into the shadows, Nathaniel lingered on the balcony...

Eyes fixed on the treeline. On the spot where a flicker of silver light had just vanished into the darkness.

*****

The next morning brought a storm... not one of wind or rain...

But of accusation.

The rumor sparked before sunrise and spread like blood in water: Selina had been seen near the sacred spring, the one reserved for ceremony... and Alpha rites.

"Desecration," some muttered.

"She's cursed," others hissed.

Training drills resumed in the compound shortly after breakfast, and Selina was assigned to clean the observation stands. Like always.

That's when Jennifer struck.

Selina had left her satchel tucked behind a bench on the edge of the field. She returned from the training sheds carrying a stack of drying cloths when she heard Jennifer's voice call out, loud and sweet:

"Oh no! What's this doing here?"

Selina froze.

Jennifer was crouched beside her satchel, holding up a small object that gleamed in the sun...

A crescent-shaped relic of carved obsidian and silver.

Gasps echoed from every side.

"That's from the High Altar," one of the elders muttered. "It's sacred."

Jennifer turned, wide-eyed and innocent. "I just found it in her bag."

Selina's mouth went dry.

"I didn't… "

"Enough," barked a voice. Alpha Bradley strode toward them, face dark with fury. "Bring her forward."

Strong hands seized Selina's arms. She didn't resist. She couldn't.

The relic was held before her like a weapon. Her satchel dangled from another guard's fist. She was dragged into the center of the square. The pack gathered quickly… whispers already spreading like fire.

Luke stood among the Beta trainees, face pale, eyes wide. He looked to their father.

Galen didn't move. His arms remained crossed. Face unreadable.

"You all saw it," Jennifer called out, lifting the relic higher. Her voice rang across the courtyard. "She stole from the altar. This is treason."

"She has stolen from the sacred altar," the Alpha said. "A crime of the highest disrespect."

"I didn't take it," Selina said, her voice ragged and raw.

"Then how did it get in your bag?" one of the elders demanded.

Selina's eyes swept the growing crowd. "I don't know," she whispered. "I didn't put it there."

Dozens of eyes avoided hers.

"Lies," Jennifer spat. "Just like her wolf. Just like her blood."

The Alpha raised his hand. "Enough," Alpha Bradley said, stepping between them. He turned to the elders. "The evidence is clear. She violated sacred grounds, and she possesses a relic meant only for Alpha hands."

"But I didn't—" Selina tried again.

"Silence," Bradley barked. "You will not tarnish this council with more deception."

Selina's breath caught. Her fingers curled into fists.

"The punishment is exile," one of the elders said, voice heavy. "Before the moon rises."

Luke's mouth parted, horror crashing over his face. "No—wait! She wouldn't—"

"Stand down, son," Galen snapped, steel in his voice.

"You know she wouldn't do this!" Luke's voice broke.

"Enough."

"You're wrong." Luke turned to the gathered crowd, his voice shaking with fury. "You're all wrong!"

Galen's jaw tightened. "Leave it. She's not your concern anymore."

Something inside Selina fractured. She didn't speak. Didn't fight. Just stared at the dirt beneath her feet as the guards stepped in.

Alpha Bradley's voice rang out. Final. Cold. "Selina Raines, you are hereby declared rogue. You are to leave this territory by sundown. Any who aid you will face the same punishment."

Selina's knees locked.

Not even Luke spoke again.

Xavier stood at the far edge of the courtyard, fists clenched so tightly his knuckles blanched. Nathaniel stood beside him, jaw locked, his eyes following her every step. Neither spoke a word.

As Selina was dragged past them, she didn't look up.

Didn't ask for help.

Didn't ask why.

"Take her satchel," the Alpha commanded. "Give her a water skin and nothing else."

A guard tossed it at his feet. He opened it, pulled out a worn shirt, a broken leather strap, and a rolled parchment. The relic wasn't there anymore.

"Strip the rest. She leaves with nothing given."

Selina stood still as the guards emptied her pack and pockets. She didn't flinch when they took the extra clothes she'd carried or the bit of dried meat she'd tucked away from the kitchen.

"She doesn't even deny it," someone muttered.

"Because she knows she's guilty," came another voice.

A low growl rumbled across the compound. It came from Luke. But he didn't move. His eyes met hers for a heartbeat before the guards yanked her forward... the crowd parted as Selina was dragged past toward the northern gates.

No one stepped forward. No one spoke. She kept her eyes forward.

Jennifer watched with a satisfied smile.

Galen said nothing.

Luke's fists remained clenched at his sides, trembling. But he didn't follow.

Xavier turned away.

Nathaniel didn't. His gaze held on Selina until she was out of the courtyard, his eyes unreadable – but burning.

The guards marched her through the edge of the village, toward the northern boundary. The same path used for rogues, banished wolves, and traitors.

Selina's bare feet stung against frost-laced stone, but she didn't slow.

Her breath rose in faint puffs. Her wrists were scraped raw from where they gripped her.

No one followed. No one called out.

Just the wind.

When they reached the tall pine that marked the edge of their territory, the guards stopped.

One of them reached forward to cut the strip of leather from her wrist... Luke's old training band, long frayed, still knotted.

She yanked her arm back before he could. Then, slowly, she untied it herself. Holding it out to the guard. "Please give it to Luke."

The guard took it without a word.

"Ama?"

"I'm here."

"I didn't do this."

"I know."

"Then why does it feel like I lost anyway?"

"Because the lie was never meant to save you."

Selina stepped past the pine, beyond the warded gates. A tremor passed through her... The moment her bare foot crossed the invisible line that marked the end of pack land, something inside her cracked.

And for the first time, she did not look back.

Something inside them had been tethered. And now, it had snapped.

A sharp jolt sparked in Xavier's chest—like fire lancing beneath his ribs. Nathaniel's breath hitched beside him, hand clenching at his side.

"Did you feel that?" Xavier asked, voice low.

Nathaniel's jaw flexed. "She's gone."

As they reached for the tether, trying to find the ends, it was gone. It had snapped. Erased before it had a chance...

Her wolf surged forward, a ripple of silver fire beneath her skin.

"We are not nothing."

The words weren't just thought. They were felt. A heartbeat. A vow. A pulse of rage and purpose.

Chapter 8 – Rogue's Moon

They gave her nothing but a waterskin and the open gate.

No food. No cloak. Not even shoes. Just the bite of cold wind at her back and the sharper edge of banishment slicing through her with every step.

Selina didn't look back. She wouldn't give them that.

She walked until the clang of the iron gates vanished. Until the scent of the pack dissolved into pine and ice. Until her calves burned and each breath dragged like gravel through her chest. The forest beyond the border was older. Wilder. Untamed land where rogues wandered... and monsters did more than whisper.

Barefoot, she stepped over snow-laced roots and sharp stones. Her soles blistered. Bleeding. Numb. Her fingers stiffened quickly, and the waterskin slapped against her hip—already half-empty.

Branches clawed her arms. Brambles tore at her leggings. She stumbled once, then again, catching herself against bark that burned with cold.

"They want you to die out here," she muttered through clenched teeth.

Ama's voice stirred in her chest. *"We won't. Keep going."*

By nightfall, the wind had turned vicious, howling through the trees like a mourning wail. Selina's limbs trembled from cold and fatigue. She hadn't eaten since yesterday. Her stomach twisted, but she pushed forward, eyes half-lidded, tracking the moon through the breaks in the canopy.

Then came the sound.

Low. Guttural. Not the distant echo of her former pack. But something feral. Untethered. Wild wolves.

Eyes glinted between the trees in the dark. Shapes moved just beyond the brush. Low, hungry chorus of growls rippled through the shadows.

Selina backed away slowly, breath ragged. Her heart pounded.

"*Let me,*" Ama urged. A pulse of power surged through her chest. "*We need them to feel us.*"

Selina closed her eyes. The didn't shift completely… but something beneath her skin answered. A flicker of silver light shimmered in her veins, glowing through her skin. Her spine lengthening with invisible strength. Straightened. Her senses flared. Sharpened.

The wolves froze.

One stepped forward, fur bristling, lips curled over sharp teeth. It snarled, ready to test her.

Selina inhaled. Opened her eyes… and they glowed. Briefly. Unnaturally. For just a breath, moonlight blazed within her gaze.

The wolf's growl died in its throat. The others backed away, yipping and whining low in confusion. Then, without another sound, they turned and vanished into the shadows.

She collapsed to her knees in the snow, breath ragged. Her legs trembled beneath her. "What was that?" she whispered aloud.

"They sensed what lives in you," Ama said. *"What you carry. Even they feared it."*

She didn't understand. She wasn't sure she wanted to. But she rose again. Slowly. And kept walking.

Her hunger gnawed deeper. Clawing, turning sharp. Her steps grew heavier, faltered. She leaned against a tree, vision blurring at the edges.

Ama stirred. *"Let me help. Follow the wind – northwest."*

Selina obeyed, stumbling forward. Her feet burned from the cold and bruising terrain, but she moved, pulled by Ama's presence humming low like a beacon in her chest. Through bramble, past frost-crusted brush, and cold stone, over a shallow ravine, until the sharp scent of water and earth filled her lungs.

And then… something else.

The scent of a hare.

"There," Ama whispered. *"Beside the stream."*

Selina crouched low, heart pounding. A plump hare nosed the frozen leaves, unaware.

"Move slow. Wait. Now."

Selina lunged – awkward, clumsy, but guided. Her hands closed around the creature. The struggle ended quickly, mercy over speed. Her stomach twisted at the feel of it in her hands. But something deeper… older, burned hotter – her survival instincts.

With Ama's help, she found flint near the stream and dry bark from a fallen pine. She sparked a fire to life, the heat licking her numb fingers. She cooked the meat in silence, the smoke curling softly through the trees. It was tough and gamey, but it was warm. It was food. She ate every bite, the warmth slowly sinking into her chest and limbs like a balm.

"Thank you," she whispered.

"*Always*," came Ama's reply.

After eating, Selina didn't stop. The warmth gave her strength, but the ache in her bones warned her not to linger. Danger still prowled in the shadows, and she had no pack now. No protection but her wolf and her will.

She pressed on.

The trees thickened... ancient pines with limbs like claws. Then suddenly, the forest opened. It was as if something had carved a perfect hollow in the dense growth.

A glade.

Moonlight pooled across the clearing like liquid silver. The air here was warmer, strangely still. Fragrant with the scent of night-blooming flowers and silver-veined moss kissed by frost. The silence was not empty... it thrummed with quiet reverence, like the space itself remembered.

She stepped into the clearing.

At the glade's center lay a fallen tree with a thick blanket of silver-veined moss and soft green ferns around it. Selina approached, breath catching. This place felt untouched. Safe. She curled beneath it, arms wrapped tight around herself. Ama pressed close, a phantom warmth at her back.

"*This is old ground,*" Ama murmured. "*Older than our pack. Older than your pain. Sleep here. You will be watched.*"

Selina climbed beneath the shelter of the tree, curled into herself. The moss cradled her like memory. Ama pressed close— more sensation than body—wrapping her in phantom warmth.

She slept.

And the dreams came.

Her mother stood beneath the glow of a crescent moon, hair shining silver-white, her eyes gentle, lit with grief and strength. Her arms reached out, fingers open. Words moved on the wind – just out of reach. A name hovered on the edge of memory. Selina stepped toward her, but the wind pulled harder, sharper, blowing the dream apart before she could grasp it.

She woke with a gasp.

The moon had lowered in the sky. The glade still glowed faintly.

She sat up, hand pressed to her chest.

"We're still here," she whispered, half to herself, half to the spirit of the dream.

"*We'll keep surviving,*" Ama said softly. "*One breath at a time.*"

Selina looked to the trees... where cold, cruel exile waited just beyond. Where the edge of the world waited.

They had cast her out.

But they had not broken her.

Not yet.

They would not win. Would not beat her. Would not see her broken.

Selina pressed her hand to the moss-covered bark of the fallen tree, grounding herself in the stillness. The wind had quieted. Even the stars above seemed to hold their breath.

Ama's presence lingered like warmth at her back—silent but watchful.

"I'll make it," Selina whispered to the dark. "I don't know how. But I will."

And for the first time in her life, there was no one to tell her what she couldn't be.

She curled into herself once more, the fire of hunger dulling behind the strength of sheer will.

The world had turned cold.

But Selina Raines would not fade into it.

She would endure.

These were her last thoughts before drifting off to sleep...

Chapter 9 – Bloodlines and Bones

Selina woke with the dawn, her breath curling in pale ribbons above her head.

The glade was hushed and golden, as if even the forest knew it was sacred. She sat up slowly, every muscle aching, and pulled the threadbare remnants of her sweater tighter around her shoulders.

Ama stirred within her… Quiet, steady. The bond between them felt stronger now. Warmer. As if something had deepened in the night while she slept.

Near the base of the fallen tree where she'd slept, something caught the light… a small shimmer out of the corner of her eye. A shimmer buried halfway beneath a mat of moss and leaves. Selina crawled forward, brushing back the damp greenery with shaking fingers.

A small wooden box lay nestled in the earth. Worn, but intact. Herbs, long dried but still pungent, wrapped the seams… lavender, ironroot, crushed moonflower petals.

Her heart pounded. Stuttered. Hands trembling, she lifted the lid.

Inside, wrapped in faded linen, was a leather-bound journal. Its cover was embossed with a silver crescent moon. Beneath it, tucked close like a secret, lay a carved stone the size of a pendant— smooth and pale, shaped like the same crescent that had once glowed over her infant heart.

Her breath caught. The same shape that had pulsed from beneath her skin the night she'd been cast out. Her fingers closed around the stone, a shiver racing through her at its warmth. It hummed faintly with power… Hers, and someone else's.

She turned to the journal. She ran her fingers over the silver imprint on the journal's cover. Something inside her pulled tight, like a thread being tugged from the center of her chest.

She opened it carefully.

The first page held only a name… Written in delicate, looping script.

Lyana Raines.

The ink inside was faded but legible. She recognized it only from an old birthday card for Luke hidden in a memory box. Lyana's handwriting. Her Mother…

Selina blinked hard. Her throat tightened as her eyes traced the soft ink strokes. This wasn't a relic. It was memory. Voice. Blood.

She turned the page.

The first entry was dated years before Selina's birth.

"To the daughter I may never hold, and the moon-marked life that may follow mine, know this: you were chosen by blood and by fate, not by chance. The goddess marked our line generations ago. Her light threads through you like silver through silk."

"If you are reading this, it means you've found the glade, it means you lived. It means the light still burns in you. Let it. Everything will make sense in time. But it also means you've been cast out—or worse. And it means… it's time you know the truth."

She flipped carefully through the pages, each one a quiet revelation. The truth poured out in her mother's voice—about the goddess's blessing and burden. About the twin-born fate. About the herbs that had been hidden, the ritual disrupted, the labor turned deadly. Selina's breath hitched as she read on, her hands shaking as each word landed like a heartbeat against her ribs.

"Your brother's soul was never meant to stay long. He was the bridge. The loss that opened the gate."

"The crescent mark is not a curse. It is a legacy. A bond forged before memory, sealed in bone, spirit, and light. Those who fear it do not understand it—and those who hate it know exactly what it means."

"We were not meant to serve the old bloodlines. We were meant to challenge them."

Selina read through tears she didn't remember starting. Lyana had known. All of it. The prophecy. The danger. The legacy. And she had tried—so hard—to prepare, to shield her child, even from beyond the veil.

Midway through the journal, a name repeated itself often: *Mira*. The midwife. Loyal, brave. A seer of signs.

Selina paused. The firelight from her earlier camp had long since gone out, but the pendant in her hand thrummed faintly... matching the pulse beneath her skin.

"Your father does not know the full truth. Not because he turned away, but because I could not tell him. To speak of the goddess's lineage in open company is treason. Even among our own."

"But you, my daughter, you are the echo of something they tried to silence. You are the storm in their sky."

Selina clutched the journal to her chest.

"I will survive," she whispered.

The words tasted like fire in her mouth. Not anger. Not vengeance.

Conviction.

She slipped the pendant over her head. It rested against her collarbone like it had always belonged there. The hum of it steadied her, like a second heartbeat.

Ama stirred in response, curling tighter inside her. *"She knew what you would become."*

Selina didn't answer. Not aloud. But something inside her uncoiled. Not Amaris. Not the goddess. *Her.*

The girl who had been cast out. Labeled cursed. Forgotten.

She wasn't just surviving now.

She was remembering who she was meant to be.

From that moment on, the glade became more than shelter. It became sanctuary. Home. Refuge. Memory. A place where she found the mother she never knew.

Each day, she trained.

Ama taught her to breathe with the wind, to run without sound, to leap power, track faster by scent, strike without hesitation. Her body grew lean with muscle. Her instincts grew keener.

The moonlight called to her. Sang through her blood. Sometimes, she would sit in the center of the glade as the moon rose, the carved stone in one hand, Lyana's journal in the other, and feel the magic hum through her bones.

She healed faster now. Could call light into her palms. She could walk barefoot through brambles and not bleed.

"I'm not the ghost they cast out," she said once, to the night.

"You were never the ghost," Ama replied. *"You were the storm they feared."*

Each night, Selina dreamed more clearly. Of Lyana. Of silver flame. Of a name she couldn't yet remember but felt on the tip of her soul.

She no longer waited to be rescued.

She was becoming her own salvation.

She was becoming the force they would soon fear.

Chapter 10 – Twins in Danger

The moon hung low over the glade, heavy with light, silvering the tops of the trees. The air had taken on a new sharpness – early autumn threading its chill fingers through the branches. The seasons had turned, again and again, since Selina first stepped into exile.

She had stopped counting days long ago, but she knew her eighteenth birthday was nearing. She could feel it in her blood. Something shifting beneath the surface. Stretching. Preparing.

Powers bloomed slowly… one after another—like locks doors clicking open one by one. Her senses were sharper now, more precise. Her healing faster. The way her skin hummed under moonlight had deepened, and the glade responded to her presence in ways it never had before – wildflowers bowing as if to royalty, the air stilling when she wept, the stars pulsing in rhythm with her heartbeat.

She was close. But not quite there.

Which is why, when the pain struck her just before moonrise, it left her breathless with confusion.

It wasn't hers.

Selina dropped to her knees, one hand gripping the earth as a sharp ache seared through her ribs – familiar, but… not. Deeper. Distant. Like her soul had echoed with someone else's scream.

"What… was that?" she gasped, her fingers curling in the moss.

Amaris surged forward in her mind, fur bristling. *"It wasn't us. But we felt it. Through the thread."*

"What thread?" Selina clutched her chest, shaking. "That wasn't mine. It didn't feel like mine... but it was real."

"No," Ama agreed. "*It was someone else's pain. Someone... connected.*"

"But I'm not... " she faltered. "I haven't... my birthday's not until the next full moon."

Ama was silent for a long moment. Then, quietly: "*The bond doesn't need your permission. It only waits for awakening.*"

Selina rose to her feet, heart pounding. The sensation was fading now, but it had left a trail behind it... like heat radiating from a distant fire. She could feel it pulling at her, urging her to run.

Without hesitating, she shifted. Amaris took form in an instant, all sleek black muscle and moonlit eyes. She ran. Together, they bolted through trees and frost, silent and fast, guided by instinct alone. Branches clawed at her face. Her legs ached. But something pulled her forward. By something older than logic. A thread. A tether. A truth rising. The same one that had snapped the night she'd crossed the border. Only now, it burned again... rekindled, searing through her like wildfire.

She crested a ridge. The scent of blood struck her like a blow.

They found the scene near the rogue border... Below, in the hollow, a figure lay broken beneath the trees.

Xavier.

Collapsed. Blood streaked across his side. Feral wolves circled him, snarling.

Selina didn't think. She *moved*.

Amaris leapt with fury and precision. One swipe scattered the pack, her power radiating like a shockwave. The ferals fled, yelping into the shadows. Her presence had triggered something in them... some old, primal fear. As if they'd glimpsed a creature not meant for their world.

Selina padded to Xavier's side, her fur brushing his skin. She shifted, breathless, and crouched beside him.

He was unconscious but alive. His breathing shallow.

Her hands hovered, then pressed gently to his side. Moonlight pooled beneath her palms. She didn't think... only let the light flow, humming through her fingertips until the worst of the bleeding slowed.

"You're going to be fine," she whispered.

The crescent on her chest glowed, faint but visible. A symbol of what he couldn't yet understand.

He stirred beneath her touch, lashes fluttering open for the briefest second. His gaze landed on her. On the mark glowing over her heart. His eyes widened, just barely, lips parting with the start of a word he wouldn't finish.

And then he was out again.

She leaned down, brushed her fingers once through his hair... then vanished into the trees.

Nathaniel arrived moments later, skidding into the clearing, scenting the air.

He smelled her.

But disbelief warred with instinct. He inhaled again sharply. Her scent, undeniable. But his mind recoiled from the impossible. He shook his head, dragging Xavier into his arms.

"It couldn't have been..." he murmured. "She's gone."

But the scent remained. In Xavier's hair. On his side...

And the ground still pulsed with moonlight where her scent was strongest... Right beside his brother.

*****

Later that night — the twins' POV

Nathaniel paced the length of the infirmary while Xavier rested on the cot behind him. Moonlight had thinned outside, but its echo still lingered in his chest. In his side.

"You saw her, didn't you." Nathaniel said at last. Not a question. A certainty he was trying to deny.

Xavier didn't answer right away. Then: "For a second. I think so."

"The mark?"

Xavier nodded once. "Clear as moonlight. Right on her chest. Just above her heart."

Nathaniel blew out a sharp breath. "But how? She's... not even eighteen."

"Maybe that doesn't matter anymore," Xavier said. "Maybe it never did. Not the way they claimed."

Nathaniel ran a hand through his hair. "Her scent... It was the same. From the border. The ceremony. I knew it. I just didn't want to believe."

"She saved me," Xavier said quietly. "Again."

Nathaniel's head snapped up, brows furrowed. "Again?"

Xavier hesitated. "The river. Two years ago. I nearly drowned during a challenge trial. Someone pulled me from the current. I didn't see who. Just a flash... black fur and silver eyes before I blacked out."

Nathaniel stilled, remembering. "You told the Elders you didn't remember what happened."

"I didn't. Not really. But I think it was her. And you know what she did on the training field... with the bolt and shield."

Nathaniel sat down slowly, staring at the floor. "So what do we do now?"

"We find her," Xavier said. "Ask for forgiveness. Tell her the truth."

Nathaniel nodded. "We need to talk to her. If she'll let us."

Xavier's voice was steady. "She saved me. Three times. Three. That's more than we ever did for her. We owe her everything."

"*I owe* her everything," Xavier whispered. "And we might not get another chance."

Chapter 11 – Mate Bond Awakens

The moon was nearly full...like a whispered promise – slow and ancient and unbearably bright.

Selina stood at the edge of the glade, staring up at the sky as its silver light filtered through the canopy above. Her breath clouded in the night air, but she felt no chill. Not anymore. Not with the hum of power beneath her skin and the steady presence of Amaris coiled within her like a second heartbeat.

She had felt strange all day. Restless. Skin tingling... every nerve alive with electricity. The glade had been humming too. Wildflowers unfurling even in moonlight, water in the spring running faster, brighter. Amaris paced within her, alert but not anxious. Almost... expectant.

Something's coming, Selina whispered silently.

"No," Amaris replied. "Something's waking."

She was stronger now.

Since the night she saved Xavier, something had begun to shift. Not just her powers, but her awareness. Of them. Of *him*. A pull that refused to go quiet, no matter how far she tried to run from it. Even when she didn't know exactly what it meant, she felt the connection. Thread-thin, but real. Vibrating through her bones.

A wind stirred through the glade, sweeping around her in a slow spiral before dying away. The air had weight. Meaning. Selina pressed a hand to her chest. The crescent mark beneath her skin pulsed once—bright, strong, steady.

And then it happened.

A pull—not pain, but pressure. Like gravity bending. Like a key turning from the inside. A tether snapped into place deep in her core. Her breath hitched.

And it wasn't only Xavier.

Nathaniel's presence echoed there too, sharp and tangled, warm and cold all at once. Like two stars locked in the same orbit. Like two pieces of a whole she hadn't realized was missing.

She pressed her palm over her heart, where the crescent moon mark still glowed beneath her skin.

"You're feeling it," Amaris said softly.

"Yes," Selina whispered. "Is it time?"

"They're calling to you. And you're calling back. The bond is stirring."

She closed her eyes. It was too soon. She wasn't ready.

And across the territory, in the Alpha stronghold, twin gasps echoed.

*****

On the other side of the valley, under the same moonlight, Xavier jolted upright in bed, breath catching in his throat. Sweat slicked across his chest. The moonlight spilled through the window like liquid silver, washing over his skin and the pendant at his throat. The one he hadn't taken off in two years. The ache that had settled into his bones since the attack was gone, replaced by a new sensation entirely.

He clutched it now, heart racing. "She's awake," he whispered.

In the hallway, Nathaniel burst through the door, chest rising and falling fast. "You felt it."

Xavier met his eyes. "Clear as fire."

"The bond," Nathaniel said, stunned. "It's hers. It's always been her."

And suddenly, so many things made sense. The pull. The scent. The dreams.

"I kept seeing her," Xavier admitted. "In my sleep. A black wolf with moonlight in her fur. With silver eyes. A crescent moon on her chest. Watching me. I thought it was just guilt. Or grief. But it was her."

Nathaniel sank into the nearest chair, rubbing his jaw. "Me too. Every full moon since she left. Every night for the last week."

"She's our mate."

The words hovered between them. Sharp. Terrible. Beautiful.

"And we banished her," Nathaniel said, voice raw. "We let them drive her out."

"She protected me. Three times... Three!" Xavier's fists clenched. "Even when she should have hated us."

Need began to consume them. Not physical, but a deep soul consuming need to find their missing piece.

Xavier stumbled to the window, dragging a hand through his hair. "She's close," he muttered.

Nathaniel raced outside waiting, jaw tight, eyes on the horizon.

They stood in silence for a moment.

Then Xavier said, "We have to find her."

"And what then? We banished her. We said nothing when they turned her out."

"We make it right," Xavier said. "If she lets us. Somehow, we make it right."

*****

Selina sat in the center of the glade, eyes closed, body still, hands pressed to the earth. The moonlight bathed her, and she let it in, let it fill her chest, her bones, her breath.

The bond hummed through her like wildfire. She could feel them now… Nathaniel's frustration like flint, Xavier's sorrow like frost. Their longing curled through her veins like smoke.

She didn't understand all of it, but Ama did.

"The bond has awakened," her wolf said softly. *"You've come of age. And so has your connection to them."*

"They're my mates," Selina whispered, barely able to believe it. Her voice trembled. "It's them."

"Yes. Two halves of the same star. It was always meant to be. To complete you when you lost your twin brother, you were fated to twins."

Selina closed her eyes, heart twisting.

She had imagined this moment differently. Some part of her had hoped, feared, guessed… But never truly believed. Not after everything. Not after what they had done. How they had stayed silent. How they watched her burn.

"What do I do now?" she asked.

"You don't have to decide tonight." Ama's voice was calm, grounding. *"But they'll come. The moon will draw them. The truth has already begun."*

*****

When they stepped into the clearing, she already knew.

They approached slowly, reverently. Not like enemies. Not like before.

She didn't rise.

"Lina," Xavier said first. Softly. Almost broken.

She opened her eyes.

"We know what you are," Nathaniel said. "We know who you are."

Selina's mouth opened, then closed. She stared at them both—tall, strong, familiar and strange all at once. Her mates. Her tormentors. Her protectors. Her past and maybe, maybe, her future.

"Do you?" she asked.

The wind stirred around them, rustling the trees.

"We didn't know then," Xavier said. "But we do now. We're your mates. Both of us."

Selina rose slowly, power radiating from her in quiet, steady waves.

"You said nothing," she said. "You watched. You let them exile me. You let them call me ghost."

"We were wrong," Nathaniel said. "We were cowards."

"We were afraid of what it meant," Xavier added. "Of what it said about us."

She studied them both. Saw the shame. The truth.

"I'm not ready to forgive you," she said. They didn't flinch.

"We don't ask that," Xavier said. "Only for a chance."

Nathaniel stepped forward. "To earn it. We'll wait. However long it takes."

Selina didn't flinch. "You want to prove yourselves? Keep my secret."

They both stilled.

"What secret?" Xavier asked.

"That I'm alive. That I'm not what they think I am. Not yet. When I come back, I want it to be on *my* terms."

Nathaniel gave a short nod. "We swear it."

"Swear it on the bond."

They did.

Selina's voice dropped, fierce and quiet: "This isn't forgiveness. Not yet. But it's not rejection either."

The crescent stone at her collarbone pulsed with a quiet fire. The moon above blazed in silent witness.

And for the first time in years, they stood in the same place... Seen, known, and uncertain.

But not alone.

And when they left the glade, she was still standing.

Alone. But no longer unseen.

Chapter Twelve – The Alpha King Arrives

The drums began at dawn.

Their low, steady rhythm rolled over the forest like thunder trapped in wood, echoing across the territory as warriors snapped to attention. The royal banners snapped in the morning breeze, crimson and silver catching in the early light as a hush swept over the pack lands. Word had spread like wildfire the night before: a summit had been called and the Alpha King himself, Kenneth Varyn, was coming. Gates unbarred. Even the air shifted, growing taut with expectation.

It had been years since a royal summit was held this far north, but the growing wave of rogue attacks along the borderlands had forced the issue. The packs were uneasy. Some feared open war. Packs were being pushed back. Borders breached. Elders whispered of something stirring beyond the known lands. Something old. Something vengeful. Whispers of dark magic returning. And still more wondered what had stirred the ferals to such unnatural boldness.

Selina stood cloaked in shadow at the edge of the trees, watching the preparations from her hidden perch above the valley. Her presence was shielded, woven into the glade's magic, but her senses were sharp. She could feel the tension crawling beneath the surface of the gathering crowd like a live wire.

Ama pressed forward within her. *"He carries moonlight on his skin. Like you."*

Selina turned slightly, narrowing her eyes.

Through the thin mist curling above the forest, a procession wound into view—all gleaming armor, proud banners, and polished mounts. At the center rode a man with silver hair and sharp, commanding eyes.

The Alpha King. Kenneth.

He looked no older than thirty, though legend said he had ruled for five decades. Power rolled off him in waves. But it wasn't that power that made Selina inhale sharply. He was tall, broad-shouldered, with a bearing that spoke of command. But something in his eyes was restless... as if he searched for something lost.

It was his face.

So familiar.

She stumbled back a step, heart pounding. A memory surfaced... Half-forgotten, dim with age: a woman's gentle laughter, a lullaby sung under moonlight... muffled and heard from the womb. But it was his image that captured her attention... he looked just like the picture in her Father's office.

"He looks like her," Ama murmured. *"Like your mother."*

Kenneth froze.

He had turned his head slightly, as if sensing something. His eyes narrowed, scanning the trees. His nostrils flared, his jaw tightened. Then his brow furrowed. Not with suspicion. With recognition. Then a whisper passed through the bond between wolf and king:

"The bloodline survives."

But before he could investigate, the warning bells rang.

The rogue attack came swift and brutal.

They surged from the eastern ridge, howling and snarling, not like wolves but something wilder. Twisted. Their eyes gleamed red with bloodlust. Warriors rushed to intercept them, but the rogues didn't scatter. They came with purpose.

Straight for the Alpha King and all of the leadership.

Selina moved before she even thought. She had felt it moments before the horn… A sharp pull, like the air had cracked around her. Amaris growled low in her mind, already preparing.

"Now," her wolf urged. *"We don't need to hide now."*

She sprinted through the trees, feet light, eyes locked on the burning thread of instinct leading her straight toward the clash.

She shifted mid-air, Amaris tearing from the shadows like silver fire. She slammed into the first rogue, ripping it from the king's flank. Her growl cracked the air, deep and ancient. Three more charged her. She didn't flinch.

Amaris danced between them with lethal grace, her coat aglow with moonlight. Every movement pulsed with a power that made the air sing. The rogues hesitated—then fled. Not because they were outmatched. But because they knew.

She was more than wolf.

She was something old.

Selina shifted back, standing barefoot between the King and the line of ferals. Her chest rose and fell, the crescent moon gleaming on her skin like a brand.

Kenneth stared.

A warrior grabbed his arm. "My King… We must move."

But he didn't speak.

Didn't move.

Just watched as Selina vanished once more into the trees a sudden pain and strong pull forcing her to move.

She found them near the river, where the ice had only half-melted. The rogues had descended like shadows, all teeth and rage, and at their center... Xavier, barely on his feet, blood on his brow, cornered against the rocks.

Selina didn't hesitate.

She shifted mid-leap, Amaris exploding from her skin in a blur of black and silver, the crescent mark on her chest glowing like a brand.

The rogues turned. They saw her. And then... They ran.

All but one.

She landed hard, claws raking across the rogue's flank, sending it sprawling into the icy stream. With a growl, she lunged again, this time forcing it to flee entirely. Silence followed, broken only by Xavier's ragged breath.

He looked up.

Their eyes met.

His lips parted in awe and confusion. "You..."

But he couldn't finish.

She padded closer, nudged his shoulder gently, then shifted just long enough to press her hand to his chest.

"Rest," she said softly. "You're safe."

His fingers grazed hers. "Don't go," he whispered, voice ragged.

Selina hesitated, then shook her head. "I have to."

She leaned down and brushed his hair back. For a heartbeat, the crescent mark at her chest glowed bright. Bare and unmistakable.

Then she vanished into the trees.

*****

The King stood at the ridge above the battlefield, flanked by two of his elite.

"She had the crescent," whispered Elder Malric, voice thick with disbelief. "The mark of the goddess. I saw it."

Kenneth's jaw tightened. "I know. I did as well. And she is the mirror image of my sister."

Malric nodded. "She's not just a girl. She's the bloodline."

Kenneth stared out into the forest, where she'd disappeared. "Then she's the one. She must be."

"She bears the crescent moon," the elder whispered. "Just like your sister did."

The king said nothing for a long time. Then: "Find her. But not by force. She will come in her time."

****

In the hall the next day, rumors swirled and crackled like wildfire. Whispers of the black wolf that glowed like silver moonlight, of a girl reborn from myth. Of crescent moonlight.

"Did you see the black wolf?"

"Impossible speed… She took down three rogues before anyone moved."

"She was… glowing."

Jennifer listened from behind the corridor wall, fists clenched. She had seen nothing. Had missed it. Again.

"Probably a trick. She's a rogue, nothing more," she muttered.

"Careful, Jennifer," Galen said coldly coming up behind her. "You speak of someone who saved our King."

Spinning around, Jennifer's mouth opened, then snapped shut.

Pleading. "You can't believe this. That *she* could be someone important. She's nothing."

Galen stepped forward, eyes hard. Boring into her as he spoke, "She's *everything* you're not."

Jennifer reeled back, stunned. Her gaze darted around, rage simmering just beneath the surface.

But she said nothing more.

Because in that moment, for the first time, everyone could see:

The ghost had returned. And she was no one's prey.

Everyone could see, except Jennifer…

*****

Later, she found Xavier alone on the terrace, staring into the woods.

"I heard you were injured," she said sweetly. "How brave of you."

He didn't answer.

She stepped closer. "Are you alright?"

"I was saved," he said, voice distant.

"By who?" she asked, trying to sound innocent.

He turned his gaze to her. "Not by you."

Jennifer flinched.

Across the terrace, Nathaniel joined them.

"She's back," he said simply.

Jennifer tried to mask her unease. "Who?"

"You'll find out soon enough," Xavier said, then walked away.

And for the first time, Jennifer wasn't sure where she stood.

But Selina knew.

From the shadows of the forest, she watched them all. The summit. The rogues. The King.

They were all pieces of a puzzle she hadn't fully seen yet.

But the moon was rising.

And the story was no longer theirs to write. It was hers…

Chapter 13 – Shadows Beneath the Crown

The summit continued in the wake of the rogue attack, its tone more solemn and grim. Every corner of the stronghold buzzed with urgent conversation... About strategies, alliances, border reinforcements. But beneath the surface, something darker stirred. Not all were mourning the chaos. Some saw opportunity.

Far below the main hall, in a forgotten chamber carved into the cliffside, Alpha Bradley stood alone. His palms pressed flat against the smooth obsidian altar that had no place in any sacred text. The stone pulsed faintly beneath his touch, warm like blood, ancient and whispering. A faint red glow emanating from its center where ancient runes were carved deep into the stone.

A figure materialized from the shadows, robed and hooded. Its face was hidden, voice like sand and silk. It slowly floated towards Bradley with a glide that defied gravity, its robes whispering like dry leaves across stone.

"You failed," the figure hissed. "He still breathes."

Bradley gritted his teeth. "The rogues were too reckless. They broke formation. She interfered."

"She?"

"The girl. The one with the crescent."

The figure was silent for a beat, and then the chamber itself seemed to tighten around them. The shadows lengthened, curling at the edges of the chamber like talons waiting to strike.

"She was never part of our pact," the voice murmured. "She should not have power. Not yet."

Bradley stepped back from the altar, the warmth under his palms growing uncomfortably hot. Uneasily he said, "I thought she was dead."

"Clearly, you were mistaken. And now your mistake may cost you everything."

"She's just a girl," he snapped.

"No," the shadowed figure said. "She's the bloodline."

Bradley's pulse jumped. "You said the bloodline was broken."

The figure turned away, the air shimmering faintly where its form moved. "We said we broke the cradle. But the moon leaves behind more than light when it flees… it leaves seeds."

There was silence for a long moment.

Then Bradley said, "What do you want me to do?"

The figure tilted its head slowly. "What you always wanted. The crown. But this time, you must move carefully. The king suspects nothing. But the girl…"

"She'll be dealt with."

"No," the figure said, voice low and chilling. "Watch her. See what she becomes. If she falters, we strike. If she ascends… we claim her."

A curl of shadow lifted from the altar like smoke and vanished. At the same time the figure snapped out of existence, leaving only the faint hum of dark magic in the air. Bradley remained alone, the weight of ambition now heavier than ever, the price of failure etched into every breath.

*****

Meanwhile, high above the hidden chamber, Galen paced the outer corridor.

He had followed Bradley's trail out of suspicion... something about the Alpha's tone after the battle hadn't sat right. The way he'd barely acknowledged the King's survival. The way his eyes had searched the horizon for someone not among the fallen.

He hadn't meant to eavesdrop. Not at first. But when he found himself outside the stone-sealed door and heard a voice that was not Bradley's... too ancient, too cold. He froze.

But he had heard enough. Voices not meant for mortal ears. The words had drifted through the cracks like poison: "the girl," "the bloodline," "the crown."

Now, Galen stood frozen outside the sealed archway, breath shallow, pulse racing. He didn't understand all of it. But he understood enough. Enough to know Bradley was not acting alone. Enough to know Selina was more important than he had ever realized.

Bradley was planning something.

And it involved Selina.

He moved quickly and silently back through the halls, heart thudding like war drums. If he told anyone; Denise, the twins, the King; would they believe him? Could he even trust them?

His hands curled into fists.

He had ignored the signs before. Dismissed his instincts. But this time, he would not.

Selina had been cast out under Bradley's command. Now he would find out why.

He wouldn't fail her again.

Even if it meant turning against the man he once swore to follow. The man he had called friend for decades…

The moon had risen.

And its light cast shadows no crown could hide.

*****

In the forest beyond the ridge, dawn bled across the treetops. Selina knelt beside a stream, rinsing her hands in the icy water. The glade's energy hummed gently around her, as if even nature paused to breathe.

A branch snapped behind her.

She spun, crouched low, Amaris bristling within.

But it wasn't a threat.

A tall figure stood at the edge of the glade, hands lifted in peace. His cloak bore the King's seal… A silver crescent woven into the threads.

"I come under His Majesty's command," the envoy said. "You are cordially invited to the attend the summit."

Selina rose slowly, eyes narrowing. "Why?"

"Because the King believes you have a place among us. A voice we need to hear. And perhaps…" he hesitated, "a right to claim."

She didn't answer right away. Ama stirred within her. The time had come.

She nodded once.

*****

When Selina stepped into the summit hall, all conversation stopped.

She wore no jewels. No gown. Just a plain black cloak, the hood drawn back, her hair falling in wild waves around her shoulders. But she carried herself with unshakable calm. The crescent at her collarbone glowed faintly in the torchlight.

The King stood.

"Selina," he said, voice reverent. "Daughter of Lyana. Blood of my blood. My kin."

A ripple moved through the hall. Murmurs rose. Eyes darted between her and the King.

Jennifer froze.

Across the room, her mouth opened in disbelief. "No," she whispered. "No, this is a mistake."

Denise grabbed her arm. "Control yourself."

But Jennifer was already moving, stepping forward into the open.

"She's a rogue," she said, her voice too loud. "She's not one of us! She stole from us, attacked her own!"

Selina's gaze cut to her like a blade. "You planted that relic. Burned my blanket. Locked me out in the snow."

Gasps echoed.

Jennifer went pale.

"Lies," she spat. "You have no proof…"

"Except my wolf," Selina interrupted. "And the moon that bears witness."

A hush fell.

Kenneth raised a hand. "Enough. The past will be sorted. But now, we face a greater threat. And we must decide together… Who we trust to stand beside us."

His eyes met Selina's. "I would speak with you. Privately."

****

In the King's private chamber, Selina stood near the window as Kenneth poured a glass of wine.

"You remind me of her," he said softly, affectionately. "Your mother. So full of fire it scared even me."

"I never knew you were real," Selina said quietly. "I thought you were a story."

He gave a soft chuckle. "Sometimes I wish I was. This world… it's harder than myths make it seem."

He turned serious. "You are my niece. The last of her line. That makes you heir to more than pain."

Selina looked down. "I'm not ready."

"You will be," Kenneth said. "Because you have to be."

*****

Elsewhere in the stronghold, Jennifer paced a servant corridor, her voice low and furious.

"She's poisoning them. All of them. I don't care if she glows like the moon, she's a fraud."

"You said she was dead," came a hushed voice from the shadows. "You promised she was out of the way."

"I'll fix it," Jennifer snapped. "One more move. Just one."

Unseen down the corridor, Luke pressed his back against the stone wall, eyes wide.

He didn't understand everything. But he caught that Jennifer was planning something.

And Selina was the target.

He moved off silently, jaw clenched. No more silence. No more waiting. No more watching. This time, he would act. Even if it shattered everything.

The moon watched. And with it, came judgment.

Chapter 14 – Whispered Conspiracies

The summit hall brimmed with tension as dawn stretched golden fingers across the horizon. Alphas and envoys from every bordering pack filled the great chamber, their expressions grim, their voices low. The rogue threat had escalated, and while the King held their focus, Alpha Bradley had his own plans.

The room was a symphony of anxious voices and rustling parchment. The scent of unease hung thick in the air. The long oak table, polished to a mirror shine, bore maps of the territories, lists of casualties, and hastily written intelligence reports. Every eye turned as Kenneth Varyn, the Alpha King, entered, his presence commanding immediate silence.

Seated near the King, Selina sat quietly, observing. Ama pulsed beneath her skin like a second heart, alert and watchful. It had been days since her return, and while many had accepted her presence – if reluctantly – others, like Bradley, watched her too closely, too coldly. His gaze felt like a blade poised just before the strike.

The meeting began with routine updates. Territory patrols, rogue sightings, and reinforced boundaries... the latest attacks, the casualties. Alpha Markus spoke of losses on the eastern ridge; Alpha Soraya raised concerns about resource shortages from hosting displaced pack members.

Then came Alpha Rourke from the Ironhill Pack, his face pinched. "They move with purpose. This isn't chaos—it's strategy. Someone is leading them. Guiding them with a skilled hand."

Bradley leaned in slightly, fingers steepled beneath his chin, voice deceptively calm. "If that's true, then we must lure their leader into the open. Use bait, perhaps. Something they want."

Selina's head snapped toward him. Her spine stiffened.

Ama stirred instantly. *"He knows too much."*

Selina narrowed her eyes. The wording was wrong. Not protective. Not defensive. *Bait.* Like he was already thinking from the other side. Her gaze flicked toward Kenneth. He gave the slightest nod. He'd noticed it too.

"Alpha Bradley," Kenneth said smoothly, "what exactly do you think they want?"

Bradley didn't miss a beat. "Power. Territory. Fear."

But Selina heard it... the hesitation, the flicker in his voice. Ama hummed with tension. *"He lies. There's rot beneath his words."*

****

That night, Bradley slipped away through a hidden exit carved into the stone cliffs. Moonlight guided his path deep into the forest, where mist blanketed the ground and every tree leaned inward, listening.

He arrived at a clearing lit by flickering torches and strewn with bones. The rogues waited... half-shifted beasts snarling in the dark, their leader cloaked in rags and shadow, eyes glowing like coals.

"You said the King would fall," the creature growled, stepping forward.

"He was protected," Bradley snapped. "By her. The girl with the mark."

"She?" the rogue asked, voice thick with contempt.

"The crescent," Bradley said, pacing. "She wasn't supposed to interfere. She should've died years ago."

The figure laughed, guttural and cruel. "You underestimate bloodlines. The moon doesn't forget its chosen."

Bradley's lips curled. "I don't care about her prophecy. I want the throne. She's a complication."

"Then deal with her."

"Not yet. She draws attention. The King watches her closely. While they're distracted, I move freely. I gain influence, sow doubt. And when the time is right…" He dropped a rolled parchment onto the ground. Maps, strategies, deployment plans. "The stronghold will fall from within."

The rogue leader crouched beside the documents, claws skimming the parchment. "You risk much, Alpha."

Bradley's eyes glinted. "I risk nothing. I am the storm already inside the gates."

The rogue's growl turned to laughter. "Then let us see if your storm will burn out or rise to more power."

****

In a quiet corridor lit by golden sconces, Galen hesitated outside Selina's door. The scent of moss and ash lingered in the air, a reminder of the rogues' last attack. He clenched his jaw, then knocked once.

Selina opened the door silently. Her eyes were wary, her frame still but taut with power.

"I need to speak with you," he said.

She stepped aside reluctantly. Inside, the room glowed with soft candlelight, casting dancing shadows across the walls. A shallow basin shimmered in the corner... water rippling faintly. A scrying tool, unmistakable. She waited, arms crossed.

"I overheard Bradley the night of the last attack," Galen said. "He met with something – something not human. I couldn't see it, but I heard them. They spoke of a pact, of crowns, of... you."

Selina's expression didn't change, but the air around her shifted. Sharpened.

"Why are you telling me this now?" she asked.

"Because I failed you once," Galen whispered, his voice low with shame. Then firmer, with more conviction, "And I won't let it happen again."

Ama's voice whispered through her thoughts. "*He speaks the truth. But his fear is real.*"

Selina's gaze didn't soften. "And what do you want in return?"

"Nothing," Galen said. "Only that you survive what's coming. And maybe... maybe that you remember not all of us stood idle."

There was silence. Finally, she inclined her head.

"Thank you," she said.

And this time, Galen bowed—not as a soldier to a girl, not as a father to a daughter, but as a man to his future Queen.

****

In the shadows of the forest, the wind whispered through the trees. The King stood at his window, watching the sky darken beyond the battlements. Below, the summit stirred with uneasy hope.

The pieces were moving. The moon was rising.

And war was coming. He could feel it in his bones. War. And something else…

Change…

Chapter 15 – The Challenge

The next morning, Kenneth stood at the edge of the war room's balcony as early light cracked the horizon. The scent of ash and steel lingered from the recent attacks, and Selina joined him silently, her cloak brushing stone. They spoke in low voices.

"You saw his face," Selina said. "He knew what I was before I spoke it."

"Bradley's words still echo in my head," Kenneth murmured. "He's too practiced at sounding reasonable. But there was a pause... when he mentioned bait. As if he wasn't guessing... he knew. You were right to warn me. His tone, his knowledge... none of it felt like conjecture."

Selina's jaw tightened. "Then you believe he's the traitor?" she asked. "He's working both sides. Feeding the rogues our strategies. They knew when and where to strike. And they knew I'd be there."

Kenneth nodded. "I've ordered quiet investigations, but he's careful. Too careful." Kenneth's face darkened. "I believe he's more dangerous than we assumed. And now we wait for him to move."

Ama's voice curled through Selina's thoughts. *"He's cloaked in shadow. But even shadows cannot hide from moonlight forever."*

"He's not only betraying you," Selina said. "He's planning to take your throne."

Kenneth turned toward her fully. "Then we'll force his hand. Let him show his true face."

They didn't have to wait long.

****

That evening before dusk, the alarms sounded Not one, but three packs reported simultaneous rogue attacks—eastern, southern, and near the summit itself. Cries rang out. Warriors scrambled. Coordinated attacks erupted across the territories. Reports streamed in from sentries and messengers—rogue incursions against Ironhill, Mistcliff, and Thornreach packs. And then one more...

Screams erupted from the edge of the summit walls.

A second wave. The other packs were a distraction. A gamble that warriors would be sent to them and away from this pack. Weakening the true target. But they struck too soon...

Selina was already running before the alarm bell rang.

She shifted midair, Amaris launching into the fray. Chaos reigned—snarls, steel, magic. The rogues had breached the perimeter, using secret access routes known only to the summit's council.

Inside knowledge...

Selina tore through two attackers, protecting a wounded envoy. She caught sight of Xavier and Nathaniel flanking the King, blades flashing. Ama warned her—danger to the left.

She turned. And there was Jennifer.

Dagger raised, eyes wild and burning with hate. Teeth clenched. Saliva leaking from the corners of her mouth.

Selina caught her wrist in one hand, twisted.

Crack. Crunch. Jennifer screamed as the blade dropped from her dangling hand.

"Why? I never mistreated or went against you?" Selina snarled.

"I should've been her!" she spat. "You ruined everything!"

Selina's voice was ice and pity. "You were never her. You were never me."

Selina's grip tightened, eyes glowing. "You chose the wrong side." Jennifer whimpered as her wrist was further crushed in Selina's grip.

Guards rushed in, weapons drawn, and pulled Jennifer away. She thrashed and screamed, kicking at the stone as they dragged her from the battlefield. Her cries echoed long after she was gone.

Only then did the warriors turn back to Selina, to the field, to the battered bodies of their enemies—and their traitors. The battle had ended swiftly since the rogues miscalculated their numbers. Most of the casualties were rogues. Ferals. Only a few pack members were seriously injured. But with a little help from Amaris, no one had died from their side.

Bradley's betrayal was undeniable now. Exposed by precision and blood. A coordinated attack.

****

After the battle, the summit was reconvened under tighter security. Alphas whispered behind closed doors, their expressions shaken. Selina stood before the gathered alphas.

Selina, voice steady, "I accuse Alpha Bradley of high treason for an attempt to take the crown, conspiring with the feral rogues, of treason against the packs and the Goddess. Of attempted regicide— for attempting to have me killed."

Bradley stood slowly, smirking and strode forward. "Lies. I deny them all. Do you have proof?"

"Only your guilt and your carelessness," Kenneth replied coldly. "You were too confident."

Bradley turned to the room. "I am an Alpha. You think to strip me based on speculation? Lies from a girl who once bore no wolf?"

Kenneth's voice rang out. "Then face the truth under the old ways."

Selina stepped forward. "By the right of the Goddess, I challenge you for leadership. A divine duel."

Gasps. Murmurs. The ancient rite invoked.

Bradley sneered. "You? A girl? And one that has not warrior training?" Bradley barked a laugh.

Selina's crescent mark flared with silver light. "A daughter of the moon. Your end. Afraid?"

Kenneth stood. "It is your right to refuse. But refusing speaks louder."

Bradley's eyes narrowed. "Very well."

*****

They met in the sacred arena by moonrise, a circle ringed with fire and stone. Witnesses gathered: the King, the alphas, the twins.

"Let the moon bear witness," Kenneth intoned. "The duel begins."

The duel was swift.

The air thrummed with tension as the duel began. Selina stepped into the ring, moonlight clinging to her skin. Amaris stirred beneath.

Bradley shifted fast—his wolf massive and dark, power coiled in muscle. He snarled and circled like a predator assured of his prey. Selina shifted slower, her form glowing with ethereal light, the crescent on her chest blazing like a brand.

They clashed... Teeth, claws, growls. Bradley fought with brute force, charging straight at her. Selina fought with grace and precision. She dodged, rolled beneath his massive frame, slicing across his side with glowing claws. He roared and struck back, catching her shoulder.

Pain lanced through her... but Selina stood.

Power surged through Selina like wildfire. She moved with Amaris's precision, her strikes true. Bradley was strong... But fueled by arrogance, not purpose.

She danced like moonlight, never in one place, using her speed and grace. A low feint, then a leap... her jaws locked on his leg. He bucked hard, throwing her off, but she landed on her feet.

Bradley lunged again, teeth bared.

A blow to his flank sent him crashing. Another to his throat left him gasping.

Selina shifted back, pinning him with her gaze. "Yield."

He lunged.

Selina spun. Claws igniting, silver fire flaring like moonlight made flesh. She struck across his face… three lines scored deep. He howled and faltered.

"Submit!" she growled.

"Never!" he snapped.

He charged once more, a last desperate surge. Selina waited, crouched… then rose like a tidal wave. Her full strength surged through her.

She struck his throat, forcing him to shift midair. He landed in human form, gasping, bloodied.

Selina shifted back, chest heaving, her hair wind-whipped and wild. The crescent still glowed.

"Yield."

Bradley tried to rise. She moved faster… hand raised, a flare of light bursting from her palm.

He collapsed. Unconscious.

The arena went silent.

From the crowd, Galen slowly moved towards his daughter.

Denise screamed. A raw, broken sound filled with more fury than grief. Then a blur lunged from the shadows behind Selina.

"Selina… !" Galen barked, already moving.

Steel rang as his blade intercepted the attacker mid-air – metal sparking against claw.

Selina spun around just in time to see the figure stagger back into the light.

It was Denise.

Her once-perfect hair tangled, her face twisted in fury, eyes wild with betrayal.

"You stole everything!" she hissed.

"I reclaimed what was always mine," Selina said quietly.

Denise lunged again, but Galen was faster. He stepped between them, sword leveled, his voice low and final.

"Enough."

Denise faltered, chest heaving.

Galen's eyes, once warm with memory, held only steel.

"You tried to kill my daughter."

Denise's lips curled. "She was never yours," she spat, voice cracking like glass.

Galen didn't flinch. "No. She's more than that. She's the future."

Kenneth stepped forward. " By royal decree, Bradley Vale. You are stripped of rank, land, and name. You, Denise Vale, and Jennifer Vale are hereby exiled. Any who follows them shall share their fate."

As the traitors were escorted away, Selina stood tall, her moonlit eyes watching.

She had survived.

She had risen.

And for the first time, no one could deny what she was:

The moon's chosen. The realm's true protector. Declared by the Goddess.

And the war was only beginning…

Chapter 16 – Shadows Revealed

The summit chamber, once echoing with tension, now lay sealed and silent under high guard. Selina's victory lingered in the stone like smoke – present, but uneasy. But the silence held no peace. Every step through the corridors carried the weight of reckoning. The traitors – Bradley, Denise, and Jennifer – were confined in enchanted cells deep beneath the keep, where even their wolves could not rise. It was the calm between storms.

Selina stood beside King Kenneth in a private chamber off the war hall, both of them facing a series of magical windows that displayed images from across the territories. Her hand rested on the smooth crescent of her pendant. Ama stirred within her, calm but watchful. She could feel it too—this was not merely the end of a rebellion. It was the beginning of something older stirring from the shadows. Smoke still rose from distant forests. Wounded messengers arrived hourly. And while Bradley had fallen, the attacks had not stopped.

"This wasn't just about him," Selina said, voice quiet but steady.

Kenneth nodded, arms folded behind his back as he stepped beside her, his silver-threaded cloak brushing hers. "Bradley was a pawn. Ambitious and dangerous, but a pawn nonetheless. The true power behind him... we need to find it."

Selina turned toward him. "Then we start with the traitors."

****

In the depths of the fortress, beneath layers of spell-etched stone, three figures sat restrained. Bradley, now stripped of his title, in chains, flanked by two of the King's guard. Denise, eyes hollow with rage. And Jennifer, silent and burning with resentment. Both with pale faces. They had been brought to the interrogation room. The room was domed and dim, lit only by lanterns etched with ancient runes. The council sat in a semicircle, with two chairs raised on a platform from which the King and Selina to preside.

The air crackled with enchantments as the King entered with Selina beside him, flanked by elite guards and the royal interrogator.

Bradley sneered looking at Selina. "Come to gloat?"

Selina said nothing. Kenneth motioned to the interrogator.

A light flared, compelling truth. The questioning began.

"Alpha Bradley Vale," Kenneth began, "you have been found guilty of high treason, conspiracy, attempted regicide, and crimes against the Goddess's chosen. Do you deny these charges?"

Bradley smirked. "I deny your right to judge me. The throne was never yours to hoard."

"You plotted with the rogues," Kenneth said coldly. "And more than that, you allowed dark magic into our realm. Who is the cloaked figure you met in the Hollow Veil?"

Bradley's expression flickered... just briefly.

"I don't know what you're talking about."

Selina stepped forward. "We heard the voice during the attack. And I've seen its mark in the magical residue at the altar in the cliffs."

Kenneth nodded to a guard, who dropped a bundle onto the stone floor... Maps, orders, and sigils taken from Bradley's personal chambers. Among them, a dark pendant still humming with corrupted magic.

Bradley's mask slipped.

At first, Bradley deflected. Then he twisted facts. But when Selina stepped forward, glowing faintly with divine resonance, his control cracked.

"Who did you meet in the caverns?" she asked.

Bradley's smirk faltered. "A shadow. A priest of something older than your precious Goddess. He offered me a way forward," he snarled. "A path to power when your bloodlines failed us. You let the realm rot under traditions too old to protect us. I did what I had to do."

Kenneth leaned forward. "Name it."

"The Hollow Veil," Bradley whispered. "An order thought extinct. But they linger in the forgotten places. Feeding on prophecy and fear."

Selina felt the chill crawl over her skin. Ama stirred uneasily.

"They said the crescent was a lie. That the bloodline could be broken. That I could take the throne in the chaos."

Denise shouted, "He believed them! He thought they would make him King!"

Jennifer spat, "And you all believed *her*."

The King raised his hand. "Enough."

"Who is he?" Kenneth pressed.

Bradley hesitated. Then: "He calls himself Morven. A priest of the Forgotten Moon."

Gasps echoed in the chamber.

Selina's heart clenched. Ama's voice turned sharp. *The Forgotten Moon… the exiled one. The god who broke the moon's law.*

Kenneth's voice cut like ice. "You brought a banished entity into our sacred lands."

"He gave me an army," Bradley spat. "He promised a new age. Without you. Without her."

Selina stepped forward, moonlight flaring in her eyes. "And what would that age look like? Blood in the rivers? Ferals roaming free?"

Bradley sneered. "Better than bowing to a girl who should've died at birth."

Galen, watching silently until now, surged forward. "That girl is more than you'll ever be."

"Enough," Kenneth said. "Bradley Vale, by your own admission, and by the evidence presented, you are hereby stripped of your name, your title, your lands. You will be exiled with the others to the deadlands beyond the Broken Pass. Should you ever return, your life is forfeit."

Bradley didn't struggle. He only smiled. "You think this is the end?"

Kenneth stared him down. "No. But it is your end."

Denise and Jennifer were brought forward next. Denise wept bitterly, swearing she had only acted out of loyalty to her mate. Jennifer remained silent, her eyes filled with quiet loathing.

"You plotted to assassinate the Moon's chosen," Kenneth said. "You betrayed the very pack that raised you."

Selina stepped forward, voice strong. "You're not just traitors. You are poison. You sought to spill blood not for justice, but out of envy. That ends here."

Jennifer glared. "You'll regret sparing us."

"I'm not sparing you," Selina said coldly. "I'm setting you free. Let the wild judge you now… *The same mercy you bestowed upon me.*"

Kenneth's decree rang through the chamber: "By royal order, Denise Vale and Jennifer Vale, you are exiled alongside Bradley Vale. You are forbidden from crossing any border under my banner."

Kenneth raised a hand. Three elder wolves stepped forward, each bearing staffs etched with sacred lunar runes. The branding ceremony began.

One by one, Bradley, Denise, and Jennifer were dragged into the center of the chamber. Each was forced to their knees as the lunar elders chanted in the old tongue. Ribbons of silvery-blue magic coiled in the air, descending in tendrils toward the traitors.

The runes branded them each on the shoulder with a sigil that shimmered briefly, then faded into their skin like a ghostly burn.

"It is done," one of the elders intoned. "You are marked. The lands will know you. No border shall open to you. No pack shall shelter you. And should you cross the sacred lines again... the land itself will rise against you."

Bradley snarled through clenched teeth. Denise wept. Jennifer stared straight ahead, unblinking.

The guards dragged them from the chamber, screaming and snarling.

And then, silence.

The trio would be exiled by the new moon, their names struck from all records. But their words left unease behind.

******

Later, Selina sat beside the King in the private solar, the fire casting shadows across the walls. The air was quiet, heavy with aftermath.

"You did well," Kenneth said. "Not just today, but always."

Selina glanced at him. "It doesn't feel like a victory."

"It rarely does. But it is a beginning."

She nodded. "Morven... he won't stop."

"No," Kenneth agreed. "But now we know his name. And you are not alone."

In the forest beyond the keep, the moon rose high, casting pale light over a realm scarred but healing.

Selina stood beneath it, hand over her glowing crescent mark.

This war was far from over.

But she was ready. And she was no longer walking into it alone.

Chapter 17 – Shadows in the Veil

Deep in the forgotten forest beyond the Broken Pass – where even the starlight dared not shine – embers smoldered in a crude ring of stones, casting eerie light over twisted roots and torn banners. The rogue camp pulsed with rot and madness, shadowy figures moving like wraiths beneath skeletal boughs that bent as if listening.

The fire hissed as Morven stepped forward from the shadows, shedding his cloak. Now fully revealed, he was nothing short of unnerving. Pale, ageless skin shimmered faintly in the moonlight, stretched taut over sharp cheekbones, as if sculpted from bone itself. A cracked crescent moon glowed red on his brow, pulsing with a dim, unnatural light. His eyes were pits of ink, swirling with something ancient and cruel. A tall frame that seemed neither alive nor dead. His robes drifted like smoke, never quite touching the ground. His eyes were pits of ink, swirling with something ancient and cruel.

Before him knelt a dozen rogues. Feral and wild, their bodies half-warped by dark rituals. They trembled not from fear, but from the weight of his power.

Around him, ferals shrank back, even those barely clinging to their sanity. He passed them as one might pass insects... beneath notice.

He stood before a charred effigy of a crescent moon, arms crossed as Bradley's report echoed in his mind. The duel. The girl. The mark. All of it pointed to a single failure.

Morven's voice slithered like smoke through the clearing, curling around the minds of the rogues like a cold mist. Several ferals twitched involuntarily, eyes glazing for a breathless moment before focusing again—as though something unseen had tugged at their will. The clearing grew still, unnaturally quiet, their chaotic snarls fading into trembling silence under his unseen grip. Even Fenric, hulking and defiant, dipped his head slightly. Not from respect, but instinctive submission to the force that pressed upon them all like a rising tide of shadow.

"She is more powerful than we believed. More than a bloodline," Morven hissed into the silence. "And now she bears not only the goddess's favor, but the King's protection."

A ripple of growls answered.

"Bradley failed."

A low growl rippled through the gathered ferals.

He raised a hand and summoned forth a sphere of blood-red magic. Within it, an image flickered: Selina standing in the summit hall, moonlight shimmering over her skin.

"The Lunar Eclipse approaches in eleven days," he whispered. "And with it, a chance to sever her from the divine."

A new figure stepped forward from the edge of the firelight. A monstrous rogue. Taller. Armored in bone and worn leathers. Eyes rimmed in silver, glowing a deeper red than the others. Intelligent. Hungry. Cruel. Violent. His face marked by a twisted alpha brand – corrupted and warped by unspeakable deeds.

"Let me hunt her," he said. His voice was gravel, broken by time and violence. "Let me tear the goddess's vessel from her bones. We are ready," the creature rasped. "We will bring the blood to fuel the ritual."

Morven turned slowly. "And what will you do that the traitor could not?"

"I was an Alpha once," the beast growled. "I know how to lead… and how to kill them."

Morven studied him, then raised a hand. Shadows curled around his fingers like serpents.

"Very well… Fenric. You shall lead the next wave. But not with teeth alone."

He stepped closer to the fire. "On the night of the lunar eclipse, the veil will thin. With it, we shall sever her bond to the Moon entirely. She will fall. Her power, mine to claim."

Fenric bowed his head, but the fire glinted off his twisted grin. Behind him, a smaller rogue shifted nervously, brushing against his shoulder. In a flash, Fenric lashed out – claws raking the rogue's side with brutal precision. The creature yelped and crumpled to the dirt, whimpering. Fenric didn't even glance back, his eyes fixed on Morven. "Weakness has no place in our pack," he growled, voice thick with contempt. The others fell utterly silent.

"And what of the King?" he asked.

Morven's cracked crescent flared. "He is only a man. And men bleed."

Morven nodded. "Then go. Gather the stones. Prepare the altar. When the moon turns red, she will kneel."

Lightning cracked above the trees.

And the war truly began.

****

The royal gardens were hushed in twilight, the scent of nightblooming flowers curling through the hedges like a lullaby. The full moon had yet to crest the sky, but its promise lingered in the breeze, casting silver light across the polished stone paths. Fireflies flickered between the branches of silverleaf trees, casting soft light across the cobbled path.

Selina stood in the royal gardens, near the central fountain, her fingers brushing the petals of a blue starflower. Her heart was still heavy from the exile, from Bradley's confession... and from the name Morven.

King Kenneth stood beside her, his face heavy with unspoken truths. He studied her profile for a moment before speaking. "You look like her."

Selina turned slightly. "My mother."

He nodded. "Lyana. My younger sister. She vanished twenty years ago during an ambush near the Whispering Vale. We found no body... only blood and torn silk. I thought she was lost. But when I saw you at the summit... it was like seeing a ghost."

Kenneth reached into his cloak and withdrew a small velvet pouch. Inside lay a crest of moonstone and silver – the royal sigil entwined with the mark of the priestess line. The Cresent Court. It shimmered like memory made solid. "This was hers... your mother's. It belongs to you now," he said softly.

Selina took the crest reverently, her fingers trembling, curling around the cool stone. A piece of herself clicked into place.

Emotion swelled in Selina's chest. Ama whispered softly, *"The moon remembers its own."*

Kenneth turned to her. "She must have found her mate after we thought her lost and decided to stay hidden, hiding you in the process. You are the last of her line. The blood of the Crescent runs through you."

Selina swallowed hard, and in a voice low and sure said "Then I'll protect it. I'll end this... for her. For all of us."

She hesitated. "There's something else... I've heard whispers. Of the Order of the Hollow Veil. Bradley wasn't lying... They're real. They've corrupted ferals, shattered borders. And if what Morven said is true... they're preparing a ritual."

Kenneth's expression darkened. "Old magic. Banished centuries ago. Priests who sought to twist the moon's gift for their own ends. Most were thought destroyed. But if Morven is truly one of them... Old court records speak of them—priests who walked between the Moon and Shadow. They were cast out by the Lunar Council long before my reign. No one's seen them in a century."

" They're back. He's planning something for the eclipse," Selina said. "Something meant to break me," Selina said. "And they're not just trying to kill me. They want to sever my bond."

Kenneth nodded. "Which would kill Ama, and possibly undo everything the goddess placed within you. We must strike first. We'll form a strike team – yourself, the twins, Galen, and a few I trust with my life. We'll find this place... and destroy it."

Selina looked up at the moon, its glow steady, a waxing gibbous moon hanging low in the sky, then she rose beside him. "A small team. One that can move without drawing notice."

"You'll have my seal. Choose your team... Those you trust with your life. I will authorize it immediately."

She touched the pendant at her throat. "They're preparing a ritual. So will we. This time, we bring the fight to him," she whispered.

Kenneth nodded. "We end them before the moon is swallowed. "Beginning tomorrow, we have nine days to finish this. Nine days before the moon turns red. If we fail... it's not just my family who falls. The bond between this realm and the goddess could unravel. Magic will turn wild. The balance will shatter. And all who call this land home – will be prey..."

Far above them, the first stars pierced the dusk. And in the garden's stillness, something stirred.

Hope.

And the certainty of war.

The final hunt had begun.

Chapter 18 – Oaths and Embers

The war room beneath the royal stronghold had once been used for ancient gatherings. Its obsidian walls carved with the runes of the First Pack, its floors etched with phases of the moon in a never-ending circle of time. Shadows clung to the corners like old whispers of the past, firelight dancing across silver-gilded columns. Now, the moon circle pulsed with renewed purpose as Selina stood at its center, flanked by firelight and fate.

Her fingers traced the edge of the etched crescent at the table's center, the cool stone buzzing faintly beneath her skin as if it recognized her blood. Around her, the selected few waited in heavy silence. The twins stood to her left – silent, solemn, and watching her with that look that still unsettled her: devotion wrapped in regret. Xavier's shoulders were tense, his hands clasped behind his back. Nathaniel's jaw was clenched, unreadable.

Galen leaned near the stone archway with his arms crossed, his eyes sharp beneath a furrowed brow. The protective watchfulness of a seasoned warrior clung to him like a second skin. And then there was Luke – her brother – newly returned and freshly promoted by the King's decree to the royal guard. He stood beside her like a shadow at her back, protective and proud. One hand resting on the hilt of his sword.

Galen's voice was low, a thread of warning beneath the question, but also concern. "Are you certain about this?"

Selina nodded. "We cannot wait for them to strike again. If we don't find their stronghold before the eclipse, they'll complete whatever ritual Morven's preparing… and I won't survive it."

She turned to the map spread before them. An old hide drawn with enchanted ink that shimmered faintly under the torchlight. A constellation of marked sites pulsed faintly in the enchanted moonlight silver ink, their arrangement forming a subtle crescent. "The last confirmed sightings of their scouts. It's an arc, like they're guarding something... Or herding prey toward a central point."

"They're drawing us in," Luke said, eyes narrowing. "Like wolves circling a den, pushing the herd toward a kill zone."

"Then we'll meet them head-on," Xavier said, stepping forward. "And destroy them from the inside."

Selina allowed a small smile. His confidence hadn't dimmed, even in the face of nightmares and bloodshed.

But then her gaze flicked to Nathaniel. He hadn't spoken much since being summoned. He simply watched her with storm-blue eyes, haunted by memory and possibility. Jaw clenched as if fighting an inner war. His silence was heavy with meaning, his energy a quiet current of need and remorse. She met his gaze.

"We're with you," he said softly. "We should have said that before."

Selina's breath caught. Her fingers curled slightly against the table. "You left me," she said, her voice barely a whisper.

"We thought we were protecting you," Xavier said quickly, stepping beside his brother. "But we were wrong. You didn't need shielding—you needed to be stood beside."

Nathaniel's voice dropped lower. Was quieter. "We dreamt of a black wolf long before we met you. When we were still boys.

The moon mark, the eyes… You were always meant to be ours. We were just too blind to understand."

Selina shook her head slowly, emotion tightened her throat, the aching mix of love and fury, of longing and betrayal. "You don't get to say that. Not yet. I care for you. I won't pretend I don't. But forgiveness takes time. You don't get to skip the hurt and rush it just because fate said we're meant to be together."

Nathaniel stepped back, accepting the line drawn. "Then we'll wait. We'll fight beside you. And when you're ready… we'll be here. We'll give you however long you need… years if that's what you need."

Luke raised a brow from beside her, breaking the tension with a dry snort. "About time you both stopped acting like moon-dazed idiots."

There was a tense pause… then a soft laugh from Selina, and it broke the heaviness like sunlight through clouds.

"Alright," she said. "Let's focus."

She gestured to the runes again. "We leave at dawn. The cloaked figure – Morven – called himself one of the Hollow Veil. The King thinks their stronghold is somewhere near the Ghostspire Valley."

"Which means blood wards," Galen added grimly. "Wards that drain magic and amplify pain. We'll need protections… Old ones."

"I've already spoken with the court's archivist," Selina said. "There are glyphs… Markings of the First Moon… that can repel shadow rot. I'll need each of you to wear them. I'll prepare them before we leave."

Luke reached into his coat and placed a worn slip of paper on the table. The ink was faded, but the crescent sigil still burned faintly. "There's more. When I was stationed near the western reaches last year, we found a ruin bearing the mark of the Goddess's Trial… a place where moon-touched warriors once faced visions before battle. It might amplify your power… or show us something we've missed."

Selina stepped closer, studying the mark. Ama stirred within her, pleased, a purr of recognition in her mind.

"*This was part of the prophecy,*" Ama whispered. "*The Trial of Flame and Frost. She who bears the crescent must walk the veiled path to awaken the old blood.*"

Selina's heart beat faster, heat stirring in her limbs. She looked at the others, her voice low but clear. "Then we go there first. The goddess is showing us the path."

Nathaniel nodded solemnly. "One more thing," he said. "When we find the Order… don't hold back. Prophecy or not, they don't deserve mercy."

"I won't," Selina said. Her voice was steel wrapped in moonlight.

As the meeting broke and the others drifted away to prepare, Selina lingered in the room, standing once more at the center of the ancient sigil. The fire's glow danced on her skin, casting long shadows behind her. Nathaniel hesitated at the door, then stepped back toward her.

"May I?" he asked, voice low, hand lifted halfway.

She gave a slow nod, heart thudding.

He stepped in, brushed a strand of hair from her face, and pressed a kiss... Gentle and reverent... To her brow. Xavier appeared beside him, his presence grounding. He took her hand and pressed a kiss to her knuckles, soft and silent.

"We'll earn your trust back," Xavier whispered.

"You'll fight beside me," she replied, her voice thick with unspoken things. "That's enough for now."

As the door closed behind them, Luke remained in the corridor, arms folded.

"You good with all this, little moon?"

Selina exhaled, the weight of leadership pressing against her bones. Her heart. "No. But I will be."

He gave her a one-armed hug, pulling her into his side for just a moment, then released her with a soft grunt.

"Then we'll all be alright," he said, and disappeared into the dark corridor.

Behind her, the runes on the war table flickered once more. Pulsing like a heartbeat beneath the stone.

The hunt was on.

Chapter 19 - The Trial of Flame and Frost

The morning of their departure broke cold and crisp. The air filled with the scent of dew-drenched earth and steel. Mist clung to the stone like memory, and the sun hadn't yet climbed above the trees. The courtyard buzzed with quiet purpose as Selina and her small team gathered at the edge of the royal stronghold... packing supplies, sharpening weapons, and fastening enchanted glyphs to their clothing. Selina adjusted the leather strap across her shoulder, securing the satchel of glyphs and herbs she'd prepared the night before. Her wolf stirred beneath her skin, restless but ready.

Selina stood beside a low stone bench, carefully painting the moon-glyphs onto strips of leather using an ink made of silver ash and powdered moonpetal. Each symbol shimmered faintly with protective energy, infused with a whispered blessing from Ama. Luke passed by, double-checking their provisions... flint, salt, dried meat, water flasks lined with protective runes.

Selina paused as she tied the final glyph onto Luke's vambrace. Her fingers lingered longer than necessary.

"If this goes wrong..." she began, but Luke cut her off with a faint smile.

"Then we raise hell together," he said as he tightened the buckle of his vambrace, nodding to her with quiet confidence.

Galen tested the edge of their weapons... each blade enchanted with sigils of resistance. Xavier adjusted the straps on his armor, eyes flicking every so often toward Selina. Nathaniel stood apart, scanning the horizon, tension coiled in his shoulders. Xavier's twin daggers sat comfortably at his hips, while Nathaniel bore a longsword etched with ancient runes. They would ride light and fast—no banners, no ceremonial guards. Just six souls walking into the shadow... unremarkable to any outsider. Their small party looked like nothing to fear. But Selina knew better. They carried more than weapons. They carried purpose.

"Ghostspire Valley lies a day's journey north," Galen said. "The old trade paths are overgrown. We'll have to go off-trail after the river."

Selina nodded. "Then we move fast. The closer we get to the eclipse, the more dangerous the Veil becomes."

They departed in silence, weaving through the forest paths like shadows. Hawks called overhead, and the earth beneath them grew colder the farther they traveled. By midmorning, they were riding hard across the highlands, the royal stronghold shrinking behind them. Wind tangled through Selina's hair, her thoughts stretched taut between purpose and prophecy. The road twisted through pine forests and moon-dappled clearings. As midday approached, the terrain shifted... pine gave way to stone, and the earth sloped down into valleys thick with mist... until it gave way to broken ridges and forgotten paths.

By the time the moon rose behind a veil of pale clouds, they stood at the edge of an ancient clearing... the ruins came into view... Jagged spires of obsidian and ice, rising from the earth like the bones of some ancient beast. Charred stones rose like broken teeth from the earth, and the air hummed with latent power. The ruins of the trial site stood just beyond, half-swallowed by ivy and moss.

They had arrived.

But they were not alone.

The air shifted—foul and wrong. The scent of blood and shadow. A low growl broke the silence. Half-shifted figures melted from the trees—rogues, their bodies twisted by shadow, their eyes glowing like embers. At their center stood a larger beast, thickly muscled and drooling with hunger.

"Ambush!" Luke shouted, drawing his sword.

"Guardians," Ama whispered. *"They once protected this place. Were chosen… but have become twisted by the Hollow Veil. Their duty defiled."*

Selina barely had time to respond before they attacked.

From the broken columns emerged a pack of rogues, surging forward. Their eyes glowing crimson, fangs bared, claws slick with old blood. They charged without warning. Steel rang against fang. Fire lit the edge of Xavier's blade. Galen met the charge with a roar, blade flashing. Moved like a storm, cutting through enemies with brutal precision. Luke moved beside him, their rhythm like a practiced dance. The twins flanked Selina, blades cutting through darkened flesh.

Selina focused her breath. Her hands lifted, the glyphs on her forearms glowing silver. She slammed them to the earth. Selina danced through the rogues, Ama's strength coiled in her limbs. With every strike, her crescent flared brighter. Nathaniel fought at her back, the two of them moving in sync, a storm forged of flame and frost.

One rogue lunged at her from the side—but Luke intercepted, blade slicing clean through sinew with a furious roar.

Selina turned, raising her hand with her palm facing the rogues. "By the light of the first moon—burn!"

A shockwave of moonfire blasted outward, searing the nearest rogues with divine flame. They screamed and staggered back, buying precious seconds for them to slip through toward the altar beyond.

As the last rogue fell, twitching in the dust from the moonfire, silence returned. Xavier wiped blood from his cheek. "They were definitely guarding this place. But by divine order or Morven's?"

Selina shrugged, unsure, then turned to the entrance of the ruin. Up the narrow, vine-choked steps she climbed, toward the ancient stones that stood in a circle of carved flame and frost. The Trial's gate shimmered like a veil of starlight. Ama stirred in her chest, guiding her. Her team following close behind.

"I go alone from this point. The Trial awaits." she said, her voice steady.

Galen stepped forward. "Selina—"

"It's part of the prophecy. Flame and frost. A path only I can walk."

She stepped beneath the arch... into the circle.

The world tilted. Darkness swallowed her.

She awoke in a dream of fire, standing in a realm between realms. The air glowed silver-blue. Ice and fire danced along the walls of a vast cavern. At the far end, a mirrored pool reflected not her body—but her soul. Her true self. Floating next to her, was Amaris.

Suddenly darkness again consumed her, before a beam of silver moonlight casts upon her skin. Then emerging from the shadows...

The Goddess.

She looked like Selina and yet not. Her form shimmered with starlight, her hair long and silver, her gaze endless.

"You've come," she said. "At last."

Selina bowed her head. "I seek the power to stop them. To protect my people."

"You seek truth," the goddess whispered. "Then face it."

Visions slammed into her.

Two paths. One of fire, flickering and wild. One of frost, silent and still.

"Choose," the goddess's voice echoed.

Selina looked between the two... then carefully placed one foot onto each path...

"I walk both," she whispered. "Because no part of me will be left behind."

From the fire rose a vision... Her mother, cloaked in moonlight, tears on her cheeks. "You are more than fate," she whispered. "You are choice."

The trees around her burned but gave no heat. Flames danced like wraiths, whispering her name. Frost swept in across the field glittering like spilled stars. Silent. Freezing ash midair. Fire met frost, and in the center of the frost rose another... Her infant twin, swaddled in shadows, reaching for her.

Pain lanced her heart. Loss, longing. The weight of what should have been. "Do not forget him," the cold whispered. "Even broken bonds echo."

Her birth. Her mother's cry. The severed bond that left her twin cold in the cradle beside her. Galen's grief. Bradley's betrayal. The Alpha King mourning his sister beneath a tree of white blossoms.

The path split. One of fire, one of frost.

Selina stepped forward, barefoot now. She walked both. Let both burn her. Let both freeze her. Her scream rang through the trial… Not in pain, but defiance.

Then came futures—war. Blood. A world cloaked in Veil rot. Her friends falling. Her mates broken. All if she failed.

Selina dropped to her knees, gasping.

"I can't… "

"You can," the goddess said, stepping forward. "But not alone."

She touched Selina's brow.

Flame filled her.

Frost steadied her.

And her wolf – Ama – howled. Purred. The goddess had accepted her. Accepted them. She had survived the Trial. And now, the real war could begin.

Selina stood, light pouring from her eyes.

She was the vessel. She was the blade. She was the moon reborn.

She emerged hours later… near dawn, skin steaming with frost and flame, the crescent on her chest blazing like a star. When she stumbled back through the veil, the rogues were gone. Ash littered the earth. Her allies stood panting and bloodied, but alive.

The moment Selina stepped out of the Trial site, the world seemed to still. They turned to her and stared… as if she were no longer flesh and blood.

Selina stood tall, the residual glow of the Trial still clinging to her like the echo of moonlight. Her hair shimmered with strands of silvery light that moved as though touched by unseen wind. The crescent mark over her heart pulsed with silver fire, steady and calm. Her skin radiated with a quiet luminescence, like moonlight in human form. Her eyes gleamed softly, the memory of the goddess etched into her gaze. For a long moment, no one moved. No one spoke.

Galen dropped to one knee first, head bowed in instinctive reverence, sword lowered. Silent. In awe.

Xavier followed, murmuring, "Moon above…" before kneeling.

Even Luke stared, stunned. Ever her skeptical protector, paused with wide eyes before giving a short nod of respect, then dropping to his knee. "Damn, Little Moon… you really did it."

Nathaniel stepped forward, whispered, his storm-blue eyes locked onto hers. "You're… glowing."

The crescent on her chest burned with silver light. Her hair glowed like moonfire. And in her eyes, the memory of the goddess shone. Selina offered a faint smile, her voice gentle but firm. "Then let it light the way."

She glanced around at the others… bruised, bloodied, but standing. "I'm still me," she said softly, eyes scanning her team. "I'm still Selina. I promise. Don't kneel."

The words broke the spell. Tension released like a breath held too long. They all slowly stood. Moving to form a small circle around her.

"Prove it," Luke muttered, handing her a waterskin. "Selina always hated the taste of sagewater."

She took a sip and grimaced. "Still do."

They laughed—relieved, uncertain, but warmed by her steady presence.

Luke was the first to move, offering a curt nod as if shaking off awe. "Good. Because we still have a war to finish."

"We move now," she said. "We end this."

And the hunt began anew…

Nine days until the eclipse. Eight days to end it all…

Chapter 20 – War Path

They began their descent from the high ridges near the Trial site, pushing northward into the ever-darkening forests. The air grew colder, thicker, with each mile. Mist coiled around their ankles like watchful spirits. Overhead, trees bent closer, whispering warnings.

That night, they camped a short distance from the Trial site, choosing higher ground nestled in a ring of stone and frost-rimed trees. A small fire crackled at the center of their circle, casting long shadows as the moon climbed high overhead. Selina sat on a smooth rock, cleaning the runes on her gauntlets while Ama lay quiet within her. The others rested nearby, Galen and Luke on watch, while the twins prepared a simple meal from their remaining supplies.

Nathaniel approached first, offering her a bowl of stew. "I can't promise it tastes good," he said, kneeling beside her. "But it's warm."

Xavier followed with a blanket, draping it gently around her shoulders. "We've been waiting for a quiet moment. Thought we'd find one."

Selina accepted the stew with a nod and took a slow sip. "You're lucky I'm starving."

Nathaniel sat across from her, gaze steady. "You meant what you said? That you're still you?"

Selina paused, then looked down at her hands. "I think I've just become… more of me. The goddess didn't change who I am. She reminded me."

Xavier's voice was softer. "And who is that?"

She smiled faintly. "Someone who hasn't given up on you two. Even when I swore I would."

Nathaniel reached for her hand, but she didn't take it. Not yet. Instead, she shifted closer and leaned against his shoulder, letting her head rest there for a brief, tender moment. Her free hand reached for Xavier's, and he took it wordlessly.

"I care about you," she said. "Deeply. But forgiveness isn't something you can earn with a battle or a kiss. It takes time."

"We'll wait," Nathaniel whispered.

"And in the meantime," Xavier added, "we'll fight by your side."

The fire popped, and she closed her eyes, breathing them in… Not just as her mates, but as her chosen. And for that moment, it was enough.

They broke camp at first light.

Frost still clung to the grasses, and the wind whistled through the ancient stones. Selina checked the glyphs on her armor, then ensured everyone carried fresh glyphs of resistance against shadow rot. Galen gave the signal to move, and they set off… Heading northeast toward the craggy hills that would lead them to the Order's rumored stronghold.

By midday, clouds had thickened above them, casting the land in a gray hush. The trees grew denser, twisted by years of moon rot, and Ama's growls echoed in Selina's chest.

"Rogues," she murmured.

A low howl answered… then silence.

The attack came swift and brutal.

From the ridge above, half-shifted forms leapt, their howls sharp with rage. These were not the twisted guardians from the Trial… They were scouts. Sentries meant to slow them down. Their eyes glowed the same wrong red, and glyph-burn scars marred their arms.

"Form a circle!" Galen roared.

The team moved instantly. Selina at the center, flanked by the twins, with Luke and Galen taking the outer edge. The rogues struck like lightning—fangs and claws flashing, howls reverberating through the trees.

Nathaniel's sword danced with frost, each swing freezing air itself. Xavier's daggers bled fire, slashing clean through corrupted flesh. Luke bellowed a war cry, his blade cutting through the chaos.

Selina reached inward to draw on her inner flame. "Moonlight, guide us."

Her crescent ignited. silver light burst from her in a protective wave, halting the rogues mid-leap. Galen used the moment to drive his blade into one's chest, then turned to shield her back.

As Selina prepared to fire another burst of moonlight, Ama whispered: *"Strike the one with the branded throat. He commands the pack."*

The battle was short, fierce, and loud. But in the end, the rogues lay broken among the leaves, their corruption slowly disintegrating beneath the moonlight.

Breathing hard, Selina bent to wipe her blade clean.

"They're becoming more coordinated," she said. "Morven's not waiting for us—he's testing us."

"We passed," Luke muttered, rubbing his shoulder.

"For now," Galen said. "Let's keep moving."

They pressed on through the fading light, finally making camp beneath a hollow ridge on the second night. They found shelter beneath a crag of moonstone cliffs. The small clearing offered little comfort, but it was defensible. They didn't light a fire that night. The shadows felt too close.

As the others slept, Selina sat near the fire with the twins. The silence between them stretched, not uncomfortable, but waiting.

Xavier broke it first. "You were... magnificent. In the Trial."

She glanced at him, then at Nathaniel. "I'm still angry. But I don't hate you."

Nathaniel leaned forward, elbows on knees. "We'll earn your trust again. No expectations. No pressure. Just... us, as we are."

Selina nodded slowly. "I think I want that. But it's going to take time."

Xavier reached across the fire, fingers brushing hers. Not demanding, just present.

Nathaniel shifted closer beside her, offering the quiet warmth of his presence. Selina let herself lean, just slightly, against him. Not ready to fall. But willing to stay.

The fire crackled.

Their hands found hers. She didn't pull away. Not this time. The night didn't demand answers—only honesty. And in the hush between heartbeats, hope took root. Their nearness was a gravity. The bond between them stirred like smoke on wind—never quite visible, always present. Her skin tingled where Xavier's fingers brushed hers. Her heart quickened at Nathaniel's steady warmth. The bond wasn't just emotion… It was magic, woven bone-deep.

But she still wasn't ready to forgive them. Instead, she turned her thoughts inward… *They looked to her now, not just as a comrade, but something more. Divine. Destined. And yet, all Selina felt was the weight of every life depending on her.*

Ama hummed beneath her skin. *"Not alone,"* the wolf whispered. *"Never again."*

****

At dawn on the third day, they broke camp. Fog hung low across the forest, muffling the world into silence. Selina adjusted the satchel on her back and stepped ahead of the others. The path forward grew steeper, roots clawing up from the ground like skeletal hands.

They didn't get far.

A sudden rustle from the treeline. A hiss.

Rogues. Again…

"Form up!" Galen shouted.

From all sides they came – twisted forms, their skin marked by shadow rot, their eyes glowing red. These were more feral than the last – desperate, frenzied.

Selina drew on her power instinctively, light gathering in her palms.

Xavier and Nathaniel fell into formation at her flanks. Luke and Galen took the outer circle, cutting down the first wave of rogues that broke through the trees.

Nathaniel let out a war cry, fire dancing along the edge of his blade. Xavier moved like lightning, slicing through sinew with deadly precision.

Selina unleashed a wave of moonlight, searing the nearest attackers. Her crescent pulsed, calling to the divine.

One rogue leapt over the fire ring, jaws open wide for her throat – while a second rogue aimed for Selina's satchel of glyphs looped over her shoulder.

Luke tackled it midair, dragging it down and driving his blade through its chest. Selina extended her claws to defend against the jaws advancing on her. Nearly decapitating him.

Galen bellowed from the other side, fending off two at once. His arm bled, but he didn't slow.

As suddenly as it began, the attack ended. The rogues fell back, either dead or fleeing into the woods.

Silence returned, broken only by heavy breathing and the scent of blood.

Luke pressed a hand to his side, grimacing. "It's shallow," he said. But the blood said otherwise.

Selina rushed over, moving his... pressing her hand to his side. A distinct glowing. Luke flinched. Froze. A sharp intake of his breath. She pulled her hand back...

They all stared wide-eyed… at unblemished skin… The wound was gone.

Selina hugged him, "please be more careful."

Galen stared at her glowing hand, his brow furrowed… not with fear, but awe. "That's new," he muttered.

Xavier shared, "She has healed me twice in such a way, but she is getting faster."

Galen nodded, staring at his daughter in increased awareness.

Luke blinked at the now-healed wound, then looked up at her with something close to reverence. "Remind me never to question your moon-touched luck again."

Nathaniel shook his head as if to clear it, then wiped his blade on his sleeve. "More probing. Testing. Looking for a weakness or trying to weaken us?"

Selina nodded grimly. "It could be both. Six days until the eclipse…. Either way, they know we're coming."

She turned back toward the mountain trail.

"Let them prepare. So will we."

And together, they pressed forward into the deepening dark.

As they pressed deeper into the woods, Ama whispered, "*I scent something ancient. Watch the wind.*"

The warning shivered down Selina's spine, like moonlight scraping bone.

The further they traveled the more concerning the terrain became. The trees grew twisted, bark split with veins of black ichor. Leaves fell in silence, turning to ash before they hit the ground.

Ama's growl vibrated in Selina's bones, *"The Veil is near."*

Six days. Six heartbeats in the life of a war. They had to reach the Veil before the moon turned. The road ahead was shadow-choked, but Selina's heart burned steady. The moon would rise. She would meet it standing. And the Veil would break… Or the world would burn trying…

Chapter 21 – The Cracking Veil

The forest changed.

The frost-rimed trees were gone. So were the quiet shadows of the wilds they had passed through. The deeper they moved, the more wrong the world became. The soil beneath their boots squelched with a black tar-like substance that clung to their soles. The trees leaned inward—dead but still standing—gray husks with bark flayed open to reveal veins pulsing faintly with violet light. Unnatural. Otherworldly.

As they moved on further from the Trial, Selina looked toward the sky. Still dim. The goddess's light waned more each day.

Ama growled low and constant beneath Selina's skin. *"We are near the Veil. Closer than ever before."*

Luke paused, squatting beside a decaying tree whose roots bled sap the color of rust. "What in the goddess's name did this?"

"Corruption," Galen said quietly, his gaze fixed forward. "Twisted magic. Evil. Death sustained unnaturally."

Selina's nose wrinkled as the stench intensified... Cloying sweetness masking decay. The further they traveled, the more the natural world seemed to cry out in silent agony. Birds did not sing here. No insects moved. The wind hissed through hollow branches, carrying whispers that didn't belong. In the distance, something chittered... A dry, insect-like clicking, followed by the rustle of leaves with no wind to stir them.

They moved cautiously, eyes sweeping side to side, hands near blades. Every breath tasted of ash and iron. A sickly-sweet odor invading everything it touched... reaching into their very centers to try to find purchase.

By midday, they reached a glade that should have been a place of worship. A small shrine stood at its center, half-sunk into the earth... stone pillars cracked and slumped, the altar defaced. Deep gouges in the stone altar resembled claw marks... too large for a normal wolf. Glyphs of the goddess had been smeared over with blood and burned. A pile of charred bones smoldered at the base of the shrine, their reek lingering like a curse. Burned fur and the faint, acrid scent of blood rot clung to the site.

Xavier stepped forward, brow furrowed. "This was a warded site. Sacred. What happened here?"

Nathaniel knelt beside the ruins, his hand brushing the soot. "A trap. There are remnants of blood magic woven into the foundation. But something... went wrong."

Ama growled, low and feral. Sharp and certain. *"He's been here. Recently. This was Fenric's work. The trap failed. He raged."*

Galen muttered, "Only a madman would desecrate a goddess's shrine."

"No," Selina said quietly. "A monster. And he is waiting ahead."

They moved on, passing through the clearing with weapons drawn. The air thickened with every step, the mist deepening into a blood-red fog that clung to their skin and stung their eyes. Sounds warped... Footfalls echoed too long, and whispers skated across the backs of their minds.

Twice they heard low snarls in the distance – twisted howls that did not belong to any natural wolf. Luke saw shadows flicker in the corner of his eye, but when he turned, nothing remained. The further they walked, the more the forest felt like a living entity. Watching. Waiting. Hungering. Looking for a way to invade... to conquer.

That night, they didn't sleep.

They camped beneath a broken canopy where moonlight refused to shine. No fire. No food. Just silence.

That night, when Selina looked up, the moon's glow seemed thinner. Dimmer. As if the shadows were already winning. Only five days remaining until the eclipse...

She sat upright with her back to a gnarled tree, fingers tracing the crescent over her heart. Ama's presence – once as steady as breath, flickered and pulsed with unease... thinned to a thread.

For the first time since their bond had awakened, Selina felt a crackle of static between them... like wind through a broken mirror. Ama's voice, usually woven through her soul like breath and blood, now echoed from a distance, strained and distorted. Selina felt Ama falter... not in fear, but in clarity. As if the connection between them, usually as familiar as breath, was clouded by smoke.

A chill slipped down her spine.

"You're quiet," Selina whispered aloud.

"This place smothers the wild," Ama murmured. "The veil is thin. Something watches."

As if summoned, pain bloomed behind Selina's eyes.

A vision. Crashed from nowhere... ripping her from the waking world.

She stood in a shattered hall. Columns of bone and bleeding glass. Before her, Morven waited. Not as a shadow, but fully formed: skin like cracked porcelain, eyes blackened with hunger. The cracked crescent on his brow bled shadow like smoke, pulsing with every heartbeat.

"You carry her blood," he rasped. "You carry her heart. But it will be mine."

Selina raised her hand to call the moonlight – but nothing came.

"You can't save them all, child. Not your mates. Not your family. Not your world. The moon cannot shelter you in the dark."

"Then I'll bring the light," she snarled.

She looked down – her fingertips crumbled to ash, falling like sand through a broken hourglass. Her reflection in the black glass below revealing her wolf form collapsing, flickering between shadow and bone.

Morven laughed, the sound fractured and echoing like broken glass. "Then come to me. Come and be unmade. The land bleeds for me," Morven said, caressing a bone pillar. "And soon, so will you."

She woke with a gasp, drenched in sweat. Nathaniel was immediately at her side, hand on her shoulder.

"What did you see?"

"Morven," she breathed. "He's close. He's watching."

Around them, the mist swirled faster… as if stirred by something that had heard its name. Even the trees groaned, shedding strips of bark that fluttered like dead skin.

Ama snarled. *"He's reaching through the Veil. Feeling for cracks."*

*****

The next morning brought more signs.

Galen and Luke scouted ahead and returned with pale faces. "There was a team sent from one of the southern packs a week ago," Galen said grimly. "We found them… or what's left. No blood. No signs of struggle. Just… empty armor and charred bones."

"They were drained," Luke added. "Soul siphoning. Like the shrine."

Selina's jaw tightened. "We're walking into a net they have cast."

"But we're ready," Xavier said.

Nathaniel pulled a scroll from his pack. Etched with glowing glyphs of the First Moon. "The court archivist said these would reveal the path through the Veil. They won't protect us fully, but they'll allow us to see what's hidden."

Selina took a steadying breath. "Then we go. Five days until the eclipse. If we wait any longer, the goddess's light may not reach us."

They pressed on, slipping deeper into cursed land. The red mist swallowed them whole. The trees grew denser and more twisted… Roots rising like skeletal hands from the ground, branches clawing toward the sky.

As they moved, the blood mist thickened until it was hard to tell earth from air. They tied strips of cloth over their mouths, smeared with protective balm to dull the effects. Every few steps, they passed bones. Animal and otherwise. At one point, Xavier whispered, "There's still breath on these. Someone died here not an hour ago."

Somewhere in the distance, Fenric howled. A long, shuddering sound that vibrated in their bones and scraped across their minds. Trees trembled. The air grew colder still. Xavier dropped to one knee, clutching his head. Luke snarled, fangs bared in reflex. Even Ama growled as if shielding Selina from the psychic lash of the sound.

"That was no warning," Ama growled. *"That was a summons."*

The path ahead flickered... Runes appearing in the fog like starlight. The First Moon glyphs... guiding them toward the unknown.

A voice, faint and forgotten, brushed Selina's mind like wind through hollow bone: "Turn back... turn back... the light is not enough..."

Selina shivered. But kept moving.

The moonlight might not be enough. It might fail...

But her light would not fail... *she* would be enough.

Chapter 22 – Teeth in the Fog

They moved in silence that first morning, the cursed woods thick around them like a shroud. The blood mist had thinned, but left behind a cold, acrid dampness that clung to skin and soul. No one spoke as they packed the camp, not even Xavier, who typically muttered jokes under his breath to cut the tension. Today, there was none of that. The air felt too brittle. Too expectant. The Veil grew thinner.

Selina tightened the last strap on her pack and looked around at her team. Luke checked the ward stones along the edge of their old camp, activating their fading glow one last time. Nathaniel and Xavier helped Galen bind his shoulder where he'd bruised it during the last night's skirmish with a corrupted stag-creature. None of them had slept much. Dreams had become battlegrounds.

Ama, always present beneath Selina's skin, pressed close today. Watchful. Quiet. Tense.

As they moved out, the group fell into their now-familiar formation. Selina and the twins up front... Xavier and Nathaniel flanking her with unwavering focus. Galen and Luke to the flanks. Luke with his blades unsheathed, Galen just behind, eyes flicking constantly through the fog.

All of them bore the sigils of the First Moon etched in pale silver across their armor, freshly reapplied each morning with sacred balm. The enchanted markings glowed faintly beneath their tunics. Even in the murky light, the path ahead was visible now, outlined in ghostly silver runes only they could see.

As they moved on, Selina paused, hearing her name whispered on the wind. Faint. Hollow. *Wrong.*

Ama growled. *"It remembers us now. The Veil is not just torn… it's awake. It breathes."*

The day stretched long. The corrupted land showed signs of ancient ruin, the bones of what might have once been a temple jutting like broken teeth from the undergrowth. Everywhere, death and desecration. Some of it recent. Each hour brought them deeper into lands swallowed by corruption, where the very air rebelled against breath and light dared not linger. Roots coiled like serpents beneath their boots, and twisted trees loomed like sentinels of some forgotten nightmare. The moon above had lost its brilliance, dulled and veiled by unnatural haze, and the goddess's presence felt muted… Distorted by whatever force now reigned in this shattered corner of the world.

They had walked for hours in silence, following the glow of glyphs that appeared only when they drew near… Faint as breath, fragile as memory. The forest grew quieter the farther they traveled. No birds. No wind. Even the trees no longer groaned. There was only the wet crunch of corrupted soil underfoot, and the constant oppressive hum of something watching, just out of reach.

Luke stumbled briefly, coughing into his sleeve. When he pulled it back, his glyph shimmered erratically.

"They're fading faster than before," he muttered.

"The Veil's eating our light," Galen said grimly. "We're running on borrowed time."

Ama's voice stirred once. *"We are passing beyond the edge. This place was once sacred. Now it drinks only fear."*

Midday brought them to what might once have been a stone circle—its original shape now collapsed, overtaken by tendrils of thorn and rot. Blood mist coiled through the ruins like a living thing, swirling around the broken stones as if guarding them.

Nathaniel pointed to a shattered pillar. "There are traces of a seal here. A barrier. It was broken... Violently."

Selina crouched beside it, her fingers tracing the cracked runes. They pulsed once beneath her touch.

"They're trying to hold the Veil open," she whispered. "To keep it torn, feeding from both sides."

Xavier turned, jaw tight. "Then we close it. Or bury them in it."

Suddenly, Luke raised a hand, signaling silence. A low rumble rolled through the earth, followed by distant thuds... Rhythmic. Heavy. Wrong.

"Something's coming," Galen growled.

They barely had time to fall into defensive formation before the fog thickened to near blindness. Out of it burst figures—feral, distorted shapes with too-long limbs, bone masks fused to rotting faces, and claws soaked in blood. The rogues had found them.

The battle began in chaos.

Selina ducked low as claws slashed the air above her. She called and moonlight surged to her palms. Slower than usual, thick, diluted by the corruption in the air, but still sharp as judgement. Powerful. She drove it into the chest of one charging rogue, watching it explode into cinders.

Nathaniel and Xavier fought side by side, back-to-back, whirling with the ease of years spent sparring. Xavier's axe cleaved through a rogue's shoulder while Nathaniel drove his blade clean through another's throat.

Luke leapt forward with a snarl, his twin daggers flickering like fangs. He danced between attackers, precise and merciless, carving a path toward Selina when two rogues lunged for her flank.

Galen held the rear, a wall of steel and will, his sword never stopping its brutal rhythm. "They're trying to divide us!" he shouted.

Ama surged through Selina, pushing her forward with renewed fury. She dropped to all fours, shifting partially, her eyes glowing with silver fire. She rammed into the largest rogue—an alpha once, now deformed by shadow. They tumbled together, teeth and claw and flashing light, until Selina wrenched free and plunged her clawed hand into its chest, tearing out what passed for a heart.

The creature crumbled to dust.

The rest fell soon after... Fleeing or falling under steel and light. The clearing fell silent once more.

Breathing hard, Selina rose to her feet. Her arms trembled, and her wolf paced within her, unsettled.

"They're getting more coordinated," she said. "Stronger."

"They're stalling us," Nathaniel replied. "Trying to wear us down before we reach the stronghold."

"Then they're running out of time," Luke said darkly. "Because we're still standing."

Selina turned to the group. "We'll rest briefly, then move on. We're too close to stop now."

They regrouped, tending to minor wounds, reapplying protective glyphs. Galen placed new warning runes around the perimeter. And for a few hours, they dared to catch their breath.

They camped again as dusk fell. This time, the trees gave way to a ledge overlooking a wide ravine. Beyond it, shrouded in mist, stood the jagged rise of hills that marked the outer perimeter of what the King believed to be the Hollow Veil's stronghold.

It would take them another two days to circle around to the hidden pass.

That night, as the others rested, Selina sat by a cold firepit. She did not sleep. She could not.

She heard footsteps and glanced up to see Nathaniel and Xavier approach, silent but hesitant. Nathaniel spoke first.

"May we sit?"

She nodded.

They sat across from her, shadows flickering across their faces. For a long time, none of them spoke.

Then Xavier reached into his cloak and pulled out a worn piece of cloth. A handkerchief bearing the old crest of their family. He set it beside her.

"This was our mother's," he said. "She told us once that the bond we feel for you would be different. Stronger. That when we found you, we'd know."

Selina's throat tightened.

Nathaniel added softly, "We were fools to let fear get in the way. But we are here now. And whatever happens next, we face it together."

She looked between them and saw it... sincerity etched in silence. The regret. The care. Grief beneath their gazes. And hope. Fragile, but real.

"I'm not ready," she said honestly. "But I want to be."

Xavier leaned forward and gently brushed his lips across her knuckles. Nathaniel pressed his brow to hers. No words. Just shared breath.

It was enough.

That night, they didn't speak much. The shadows pressed too close. But when Selina lay back, staring at the faint glimmer of the moon through the crimson haze, she reached out to the bond she shared with Ama.

"We're almost there," she whispered.

Ama's voice responded, quieter than usual but fierce as ever. *"And when we arrive, the Veil will break or burn."*

Selina closed her eyes, fingers brushing the crescent mark over her heart.

Four days until the eclipse.

And the world would either be saved... or swallowed whole.

*****

The next morning, before they could break camp, the fog thickened again. Three days... Three days until the eclipse. They needed to move faster...

As they packed up camp again, Galen paused near Luke.

"She's stronger than we ever gave her credit for."

Luke gave a tired smile. "She always was. We just didn't want to see it."

Ama suddenly snarled... *"They come!"*

Rogues burst from the mist. Twisted, mangled forms... Half-human, half-shadow. At least a dozen, with blades of bone and mouths full of jagged teeth.

The battle exploded into chaos.

Selina met them head-on, her blades singing with moonlight. Xavier's axe cleaved two rogues apart in a single swing while Nathaniel moved like lightning, his dagger carving runes mid-strike. Luke dropped from a tree, shifting midair, landing on a rogue with a growl and a snap.

Galen moved with brutal efficiency, shielding the rear, but suddenly grunted, shoulder seizing as he pivoted to block another strike. One rogue slipped past his guard... Only to meet Selina's blade, already descending like judgment... blade driving through its chest.

More kept coming.

Ama surged within her. *"Let me rise."*

Selina let go.

Her wolf burst forth, cloaked in silver fire, crescent glowing at her heart. Massive. Radiant. The earth recoiled where her paws struck. She *was* the moon's fury, made flesh. Silver light beating back the shadows. Her howl shattered the mist.

And in that moment, her howl summoned truth. Far in the distance, the corrupted trees shuddered. A distant wind rose, carrying her howl across miles. The Veil had heard her. And it stirred.

The tide turned.

Xavier stared at the scorched clearing, breath caught in his throat. "She's not just moon-touched anymore," he whispered. "She *is* the moon."

When it was over, they stood bloodied but unbroken.

Bodies of the fallen melted into black sludge, evaporating into the cursed earth.

They regrouped in silence, each of them understanding what had just been confirmed.

The enemy knew where they were.

They were being hunted.

They set out again, weary but resolute. Exhaustion dragged at their limbs, but none spoke of turning back. They walked forward—because to stop was to die, and to die was to lose everything.

As the day closed, the hills finally came into view... Jagged and black against the near full-moon in the sky. The stronghold lay just beyond.

Three days until the eclipse. Two until the gates of the Veil...

And the war would begin.

Chapter 23 – Blood in the Shadows

They moved swiftly the next morning, the jagged hills looming ever closer with each hour. The land beneath their feet grew more twisted with every step; roots gnarled like grasping fingers, stones streaked with veins of black ichor, and the sky clocked in a pale, sickly hue. Selina felt the pull in her bones… Not just of the path ahead, but of fate itself. The moon hung heavy above them, even in daylight, a silver ghost watching their every step… like prophecy made flesh in its vigilance.

Ama stirred within her. "*The Veil thickens. The land bleeds shadow. We are close. But something old stirs beneath it. Something… waiting.*"

Bruises had started to fade from the last major skirmish, but the weight of tension grew with every mile. Even the wind seemed to whisper warnings, brushing against their skin like cold breath from a long-dead spirit.

As they rounded a ridge that cut through the rising terrain, Luke held up a hand. His eyes narrowed on the path at his feet. "There's a trail of blood here. Fresh."

Galen stepped forward and knelt beside it. His fingers touched the dark stain seeping into the mossy stones and soil. "Not animal. Rogue. Wounded. But large. Heavy."

Selina's pulse quickened. She turned to Nathaniel and Xavier who both stiffened at her side. "Fenric," she said.

Xavier nodded grimly. "If he's ahead, he won't be alone. He's too unstable to travel without chaos."

They followed the trail into a narrow canyon where the mist curled like breath from a dying beast. Jagged rock walls loomed around them, funneling sound and scent into an echo chamber of dread. The air reeked of copper and rot. Dead things littered the rocks—feral rogues, torn apart, some still twitching. Their bodies were mutilated, as though something had not only killed them, but made a spectacle of it.

"He did this," Galen muttered. "Even his own kind aren't safe."

"They were his amusement," Luke added, voice hard. "Or his mistake."

The shadows deepened, the world going still. They crept forward. The shadows thickened.

The canyon seemed to exhale—wind hissing through the rocks, stirring ash and brittle leaves. A shape moved just beyond the edge of vision. Then another.

Xavier shifted, grip tightening on his axe. "We're not alone."

The rocks trembled. A low growl rumbled, primal and rising.

Then…

A roar shattered the stillness. Shattered the silence of the veil…

A shadow lunged from the ledge above… massive and wild, blood still slick on his claws. Snarling…

 Fenric.

Bone armor clung to his limbs, cracked and soaked with old gore. His eyes burned red, ringed in silver. Madness dancing in their depths. A deep growl rolled from his chest as he stalked into view... teeth bared. The stench of rot and iron hit them before the beast did, as though the very air recoiled from his presence.

"Goddess's bitch," he spat. "You dare hunt *me?!?*"

Selina stepped forward, the pendant around her neck flashing with silver light. "I'm not hunting you. But I won't let you stand in our way."

He leapt.

They scattered.

Steel met claw. Xavier intercepted him mid-air, driving his axe into Fenric's shoulder. The blow landed, Fenric shrugged it off with a guttural snarl, hurling Xavier aside like a broken doll. Luke darted in, twin blades flashing, slicing deep along Fenric's thigh. The rogue alpha howled and lashed out, claws raking Luke across the chest. Blood sprayed across the canyon floor... mixing as it landed, before quickly absorbing into the dark soil – almost as if it were drinking nourishment.

Selina flared with silver light, her pendant burning against her skin. The power surged through her, wild and bright—but it burned too. The goddess's fury rode her bones like fire, pushing her faster, harder. A flicker of fear crept in. She felt herself drowning in the divine. Was this still her will, or something else—something holier and colder? *Am I still myself? Or something more? Something less?*

Ama answered with a snarl: *"You are ours. You are enough."*

She shifted partially, fur bristling along her arms, eyes glowing like twin moons. Ama surged within her, lending strength, fury, precision. The goddess's power filled her limbs.

She met Fenric head-on.

Claw to claw, light against shadow.

Their clash sent a shockwave down the canyon. They crashed into a pillar of rock, shattering it. Fenric snarled, trying to bite her throat, but she rolled and slammed him to the ground. Her blade sank into his side, drawing more corrupted blood to sink into the dark soil. He roared and flung her off, crashing her into the canyon wall.

Galen charged with a war cry, striking across the back, slamming his sword into Fenric's spine. The monster staggered. Nathaniel followed, carving a glowing rune into the skin of Fenric's that seared with divine heat. He began to shriek and stagger, eyes wide with pain for the first time.

Smoke rose from the seared rune on his back, the flesh blistered and bubbling. He staggered, one arm half-shifted, claws twitching uncontrollably... As though he could no longer command his own body.

Selina forced herself up, blood in her mouth but unbowed, and raised her hands. Moonlight burst from her fingertips, a radiant wave that slammed into Fenric like a tidalwave. He screamed, staggered back. Skin blistering from the light.

Their eyes met for a heartbeat—his wild and hateful, hers blazing with silver wrath. Then he turned and fled, roaring defiance, his howl fractured by pain. Disappearing into the mountains. Wounded.

They stood in stunned silence. Selina pressed a trembling hand to her ribs, wincing as pain bloomed beneath her skin. No one spoke at first. Only breath. Only the wind.

Galen helped Luke to his feet, ripping cloth to press to the wound. "You'll live."

Luke grimaced, then let out a low, bitter laugh. "He hits like a mountain. That… was not our final fight, was it?"

Xavier sheathed his axe with a grunt and wiped blood from his jaw. "And runs like a coward."

Selina said nothing at first. She stared into the shadows at the path where Fenric had vanished. "No," Selina said. "Just the storm before the dark."

Ama whispered, "*He will return. At the Veil. With Morven.*"

They moved on, slow and cautious now.

By dusk, they reached the edge of a desolate rise. In the distance, across a barren field soaked in blood and broken stone, stood the Hollow Veil.

A wall of black mist. A fortress of shadow. A tear in the world.

Selina stepped forward, her pendant glowing bright as dawn. Her wolf stirred deep inside her. Watchful. Ready. *"He waits within. The Veil hungers. And it knows your name,"* Ama warns.

Two days until the eclipse. Only one until the final battle. And already, the world had begun to bleed…

Selina pauses and looks to the sky at the faint outline of an almost full moon, *"Tomorrow, the goddess howls."*

Chapter 24 – Shadows and Claws

The night before the storm was silent.

They made camp just beyond the desolate field, a short distance from where the Hollow Veil loomed like a wound in the earth. The air was still, heavy with tension, as if the land itself held its breath. The campfire flickered against the encroaching mist, casting long shadows on the stone faces of the warriors gathered around it.

Selina stood at the perimeter, eyes on the horizon where the black fog curled like the fingers of some slumbering beast. Her shoulders were squared, but beneath the calm mask, her pulse hammered like a war drum – fast, loud, prophetic. The goddess stirred beneath her skin. Ama watched. The moon above pulsed with quiet urgency.

None of them slept.

Luke sharpened his blade with steady, deliberate strokes. Galen sat cross-legged, his hands wrapped around a warm flask of bitterroot tea, gaze fixed beyond the veil. The twins flanked the fire… Xavier rubbing a whetstone over his dagger while Nathaniel carved invisible lines into the dirt beside him.

The silence between them was not cold. But reverent.

Behind her, the others moved in near silence… preparing weapons, checking gear, weaving protective glyphs into armor and skin. They knew the battle tomorrow might be their last. And yet none of them flinched.

Selina returned to the fire and crouched beside the twins, her expression softening as they looked up at her.

Her voice low, "I need you both steady tomorrow."

Xavier gave a half-smile. "Aren't we always?"

Nathaniel's voice was quieter, more serious. "We'll die before we let anything touch you."

"I'm not asking you to die," she said. Her voice cracked. "I'm asking you to live. To live through all of it... With me."

They nodded. No promises, only resolve.

She moved next to Galen, who handed her a freshly inked rune scroll.

"I prepared the moonlight wards," he said. "Place them along the inner perimeter when we breach the Veil. It may buy us time."

Luke came to her side, setting down his pack. "The scouts report no movement yet. But I don't trust that mist."

"Neither do I," she murmured.

She stepped back and raised her hand. The moon's light caught the runes etched in her palm and shimmered through her veins. Her voice, low and resonant, carried words older than the packs themselves. A protective blessing. A ward against soul-rot. A final gift of clarity for the warriors who stood beside her.

When she finished, a hushed reverence settled.

Luke whispered, "Feels like the calm before the storm."

"No," Selina said, eyes glowing faintly. "It's the breath before the howl."

＊＊＊＊＊

At first light, they stood at the edge of the Hollow Veil. Morning came with no birdsong—just silence, heavy and expectant.

They broke camp under a pale sun barely visible through the mist that clung to the land like breath on glass...

The mist parted for no one. It clung to skin and spirit alike, as though the Veil itself wished to consume them before they arrived. Shadows twisted within it... some whispering, others screaming. The land trembled beneath their feet. As they stepped forward in formation, the Veil seemed to resist their very presence, a wall of shadow pressing inward, alive and breathing.

Ama growled low in Selina's mind: *"It sees us. It remembers what we carry."*

Selina led the way, her pendant glowing brighter with every step. The others followed, eyes hard, weapons drawn, forming a protective crescent around her. The further they walked, the stranger the world became. Trees bled sap as dark as pitch. The soil crunched like bone. Time slowed.

They encountered no immediate resistance, but the deeper they traveled, the more twisted the terrain became. Shapes moved in the corner of their vision. Whispers tried to echo voices of loved ones. Illusions clawed at their minds.

Xavier nearly struck Nathaniel, caught in a mirage of the past. Luke faltered, seeing his mother's face in the smoke. Selina alone held fast, anchoring them with a pulse of silver that seared through the Veil's illusions.

Ama surged beneath her skin, stronger now... As if the approaching moon pulled more than tides. The closer they came to the Veil's heart, the more Selina felt the divine fire coiling at her core.

They pressed on. The shadows thinned slightly, just enough for them to glimpse what lay ahead.

By midday, they reached the desecrated shrine. The sun hovered at its peak… blotted by the thick fog of the Hollow Veil… A corrupted shrine, sunken and half-destroyed. A desecrated altar. Charred and bleeding black mist.

"Morven was here," Galen said grimly.

Signs of ritual circled the ruin: bones etched with runes, stones soaked in blood, sigils scorched into the earth. And there, at the center, a twisted effigy of the moon. Mocking. Broken.

Then… movement. A blur in the mist.

Selina turned. "Get ready."

Rogues poured from the trees, snarling and half-shifted, eyes wild. But something was wrong. They attacked not with coordinated intent. But desperation. As if something had driven them into madness.

Fenric's handiwork.

The battle was brief, brutal. Selina and the twins fought back to back, blades cleaving shadows. Luke and Galen flanked. Magic clashed with bloodlust. When the last rogue fell, choking on its own fury, the air fell silent once more.

The shrine lay in ruins.

Xavier spat. "He's out of control. This wasn't strategy. It was carnage."

Nathaniel pointed to claw marks deep in the altar. "He destroyed part of the ritual. I think… he was trying to complete it and failed. Or someone else did."

Selina knelt by the remains of the altar. Ama stirred within her. *"This was meant to break something. Or someone… It was meant to break me… They failed. For now."*

"If they had succeeded here…" Selina whispered, fear tinging her voice, fingertips brushing the still-smoking altar. "They wouldn't have needed the eclipse. They would've torn Ama from me *here*."

Xavier crouched, brushing soot from a stone near the altar. "There's something burned into it – letters… or symbols."

Selina leaned closer. The shape resembled a broken moon with jagged wings.
"He left this for us. It's not a warning. It's a challenge."

She rose and turned to the others. "We're close. Two days left. We rest for a few hours… long enough to sharpen blades and catch out breath. By nightfall, we find Morven… "We strike before midnight. We end this before the goddess reaches her peak… *before* the moon begins its descent into shadow."

They continued onward, the Veil pressing in behind them.

And far in the distance, something… someone… watched.

Ama's presence tensed. *"We're being watched. Not by the rogues. By something older,"* Ama whispered. *"And it remembers what the goddess forgot."*

Selina's spine stiffened. The air itself felt wrong. *Older* than the land, colder than night. Observing them all…

The moon rose above the black mist. Pale. Patient.

Waiting.

A howl rose… Not yet Selina's, but something darker. Distant, ancient, and hungry. The black mist of the Hollow Veil shivered… like it, too, had heard the howl approaching.

Ama whispered again, colder this time: *"We're running out of time. Morven won't wait for the moon. He will meet it with blood."*

Selina's gaze stayed fixed on the sky…her face trying to absorb the faint light of the moon. "Tomorrow is no longer waiting," she whispered. "It begins tonight."

Chapter 25 – The Moon Bleeds

The sun dipped low, painting the sky in strokes of crimson and ash. Twilight fell like a blade, swift and unforgiving.

Selina stood at the edge of a shallow ridge, overlooking the Hollow Veil's core—an open basin of blackened stone and twisting fog, encircled by jagged spires. Beneath the surface, ancient ruins pulsed faintly with corrupted light, like veins beneath diseased skin… the Veil churned in a maelstrom of dark mist and pulsing crimson glow—like the land itself was bleeding from an unseen wound. The sky pale, the moon swelling behind drifting cloud. The eclipse would come soon. Too soon.

"We're out of time," Galen said, adjusting the blade strapped to his back. "If we're going to strike, it has to be now."

Selina nodded. "This is the last light before shadow."

The war party spread out along the ridge. Luke on the western rise, Galen and the twins circling the southern flank. Wards were cast. Weapons drawn. The air thickened, humming with dread. Even Ama was silent now… Watching. Waiting.

Then the wind shifted. Everyone could feel it.

And the Veil screamed.

The final battle had begun.

"They've fortified the basin," Luke said, crouching at the edge of the ridge. "Ritual stones around the perimeter. Runes I don't recognize. A circle of guards. And more inside."

Selina studied the field. Her heartbeat had grown steady, too steady. It wasn't calm... it was focus. Ama was a blazing flame within her chest, whispering in divine cadence.

"This is where it ends," she said. "We go in. We stop the ritual. We stop him."

Nathaniel touched her arm gently. "We follow your lead."

Xavier gave a small nod, his blade already drawn.

Galen grunted. "Then let's make it count."

They descended the ridge like ghosts. Wards glowed faintly along their gear—Selina had redrawn the glyphs from the Trial earlier that morning. They shimmered now with the moon's growing power, casting a faint silver light through the thick fog.

As they breached the basin edge, the rogues were already waiting.

The battle exploded in an instant.

Rogues burst from the basin fog... Dozens, then scores. Howling. Charging. Half-shifted monstrosities, their limbs elongated, eyes glowing with voidfire and madness. They surged like a wave... like shadows with teeth, and Selina and her warriors met them with a roar.

Steel clashed. Magic seared. The earth split. Selina answered with a blast of moonlight, clearing a path to the center of the basin where the altar pulsed like a heartbeat.

Selina fought at the center, silver fire blazing from her hands, Ama's strength magnified by the nearing moon. Xavier and Nathaniel flanked her, moving in tandem—two shadows sworn to her light.

She saw Morven standing atop the ritual platform, arms raised.

Somewhere in the chaos, Galen let out a shout… "Left side's collapsing!"…as a monstrous figure tore through the battle line.

Fenric.

Twisted. Scarred. Blood-maddened. His skin was streaked with ritual symbols, his fangs dripping with shadowed essence. He moved like a beast unchained. Recovered just enough…

"Selina!" Luke yelled.

His mouth twisted in a mad grin. "You made it," he growled, throwing over his shoulder as he charged towards Selina. "Good. I want to hear you scream when she burns."

She turned just as Fenric barreled toward her. The world narrowed. Ama surged. They both met him head-on.

Their collision shook the ridge. The earth split beneath him from the force.

Their clash was cataclysmic – cracking the air itself. Selina's blade and light against Fenric's corrupted strength. Her moonfire flaring, his claws tearing, both fury and prophesy made flesh. They moved in a whirlwind of fire and teeth. He tore at her wards, she broke bones in return. Fenric snarled, strength monstrous, striking like a storm… But Selina was no longer the girl who had hidden in her father's shadow.

He scored her shoulder… she shattered his knee. He slammed her to the ground… she drove a knife into his shoulder. He slammed her against a stone column… she drove a blade of moonlight through his side.

The battle slowed as warriors turned to witness the clash – Alpha and aberration, blood and fate.

They rolled apart, both bleeding. Ama screamed through Selina's throat, and with a surge of power, she forced Fenric back with a wave of burning light.

Fenric stumbled, staggered, growling, but did not fall. Grinned, eyes wild. "You are not the goddess," he spat.

She bled. Staggered. Rose again. "No," Selina panted, voice cold and low. "I am her wrath."

He growled, then fled to the shadows, his body flickering with dark energy. Turning at the edge, Fenric taunted, "Next time, little moon."

Ama roared with her – and Selina drove a pulse of silver flame through his chest before he could turn away again. It didn't kill him. But it sent him crashing into the rocks behind. Wounded. Screaming.

Before he vanished into the mist.

They didn't chase him.

Because Morven still waited on the alter… the true enemy.

Selina turned back toward the altar – during the fight Morven had begun to chant. The bloodstones flared, drawing crimson threads from the ground toward the sky. The moon had fully risen. The eclipse loomed behind it like a curtain of dark silk.

He stepped into the clearing like a shadow drawn into flesh – tall, cloaked in robes that seemed stitched from the void. His cracked crescent shimmered red on his brow. Behind him, acolytes chanted in a language that bled.

"So the child of prophecy arrives," Morven said, his voice like silk dragged over stone. "And on time. How rare."

Selina stepped forward. "This ends now."

He smiled, cruel and ageless. "You think you've won just because you wounded my pet? The moon has not peaked. The veil is still open. And you... you are still only mortal."

Ama's voice rang like a bell in Selina's skull: *"He means to pierce the veil before the shadow touches the moon. If he succeeds... my bond with you will break."*

Selina sprinted toward the altar. Galen and Luke fought to her right, keeping the acolytes at bay. The twins flanked her left, driving back rogue warriors in coordinated strikes.

The air pulsed.

Morven's voice deepened. Reality cracked.

Ritual stones surrounding the basin began to glow. The ground beneath Selina's feet cracked. Blood began to flow in unnatural patterns toward the center of the battlefield—toward a crude altar hidden beneath the Veil's crust.

Morven's ritual had already begun.

Selina reached for the runes inked along her forearms. "No," she whispered.

And the battlefield ignited... Again. More rogues... even more twisted than the last.

Galen, Luke, and the twins created a path... Clearing. Defending. To reach the alter.

Selina reached the ritual stones and drove her blade into the first sigil. The light dimmed.

"No!" Morven hissed. "You are the vessel! You should be kneeling at my feet!"

Selina raised her hand—and moonlight answered. Glyphs surged across her skin. The energy of the Trial returned to her, burning brighter than ever.

"I am not your vessel," she said, climbing the altar steps. "I am the storm you failed to read."

He lashed out with dark tendrils—Selina blocked them with her bare hand, the divine energy in her pulse obliterating the corrupted magic.

She reached the center of the altar.

The final ritual crystal pulsed... deep and red, like a corrupted heart. Selina pressed her hand to it. It shattered beneath her touch. The entire field shook...

The Veil screamed.

The tether between realms snapped with a shriek of magic so loud it split the clouds above.

Morven screamed in fury, recoiling as the ritual shattered.

"No! No! The Veil was open!"

"It's closed now," Selina whispered.

Ama rose within her, blazing through her form.

Selina's eyes glowed like twin moons.

She struck Morven with everything: light, fury, prophecy – destiny incarnate. He screamed as his body cracked stone... His shadow peeled away into nothingness.

The Hollow Veil shrieked, folding like a dying star. Mist fled. Light surged. And then... Silence.

The battlefield grew still.

The rogues, broken and disoriented, fled into the forest. What few remained were subdued by Galen, Luke, and the twins. Fenric was gone. Morven was no more.

Selina stood at the heart of the ruined altar, breathing hard.

The moon above... untouched by shadow, glowed pale and powerful.

Ama whispered, *"We made it. Before the eclipse."*

Nathaniel reached her side, bruised and breathless. "Is it done?"

Selina looked to the ruined basin around them.

"For tonight," she said. "But dawn will bring something new. A world waiting for us."

Galen approached the edge of the ruined altar, gaze scanning the torn battlefield, the silent basin, the swirling remnants of broken magic.

"It's over," he said, but there was a tightness in his voice. "But it doesn't feel *finished*."

Selina turned toward him, pulse still echoing with divine fire. "The Veil is sealed. Morven is gone."

Galen nodded once. "I know. And yet... something in the shadows still watches. As if Morven was only the first hand of something deeper."

Ama stirred faintly. *"He was a conduit... but not the root."*

Selina's jaw clenched. She didn't answer. Just looked to the far horizon where night began to lift, but not all of the dark had gone with it. Some lingered in the far reaches...

Above them, the clouds finally parted.

A shaft of pure moonlight broke through, falling across the altar like a benediction. It struck the bloodstained stones, and where the light touched, the rot began to recede—char fading to ash, black mist dissolving into harmless vapor.

The air stirred. Not with malice, but with quiet.

And from the edge of the woods, a single wolf howled. Not in mourning, but in survival. In triumph. The darkness, at last heard her name...

The Goddess's light had returned.

Chapter 26 – Dawning of Unity and Acceptance

Dawn arrived with golden quiet. Its light breaking over the horizon like a held breath finally released… soft and unburdened. The air was crisp, tinged with the scent of scorched earth and old magic. Mist clung low across the charred ground, curling like ghostly fingers around broken stones. In the distance, the final echoes of battle faded beneath the song of waking birds. The stillness wasn't silence. It was reverence, as though the world itself had paused to remember what had passed and to breathe in what was yet to come. For the first time in many moons, the sky was clear. The battle was over, yet the land still trembled with the memory of what had passed – blood, and prophecy.

Selina stood at the edge of the ruined basin where the Hollow Veil had collapsed, the ruins still smoking faintly around them. Her skin still tinged with moonlight, her hands stained with ash. Behind her, the war party moved in silence, tending to wounds, creating a pyre to tend the dead… lit cleansing flames, whispered old rites. Dismantling what remained of Morven's ritual site. The battlefield was silent. Not lifeless—only still. The kind of stillness that came after something sacred had passed through. The battle had taken much from them, but it had given something too— freedom, choice, a future.

She walked slowly to the center of the field, where the cracked altar stood like a scar across the earth. She placed her palm over the broken surface, letting the last flickers of divine warmth pulse through her skin. Ama stirred, content now, her presence woven into Selina's every breath.

A low whistle announced Luke's arrival beside her. "Still glowing like a goddess, you know."

"Don't start," Selina said, but her smile was soft.

Galen, Nathaniel, and Xavier joined them, and with them came the murmuring of others—survivors, allies, even scouts from nearby territories. Word was already spreading. The Hollow Veil had fallen. The cursed moon had risen, and not consumed them. The prophecy had come true.

And the packs were coming.

By midday, representatives from three neighboring territories had arrived. The first came draped in the pale blues and grays of the Frostedge Pack, their faces still drawn from travel, but their eyes wide with something like reverence. The second bore the dark leathers of the Ironfang… stoic and proud, yet their leader removed his helm and bowed low. The third wore moss-colored cloaks, the emblem of the Greenfen Tribe embroidered in gold thread over their shoulders. One of them, an older woman with eyes the color of pine bark, approached with a single white flower cupped in her palms. An ancient gesture of peace.

They stood in a loose circle at the edge of the clearing. Some with hesitation, others with cautious hope. Murmurs passed between them… soft as the wind, heavy with disbelief. Yet in every expression lingered the same thing: wonder. They had heard the stories, but now they stood in the presence of the Moon-Blessed Alpha. And they waited, breath held, for her to speak. Some knelt, others stood silent. All waited for her to speak.

Selina stepped onto the altar stone, not elevated by power, but by purpose.

"The prophecy spoke of ruin, of a child born before her time, marked by sorrow and shadow. But it also spoke of unity, of truth, of peace."

She looked at the assembled faces... bloodied, tired, hopeful.

"We are no longer bound by the failures of the past. No longer ruled by fear or blind allegiance to power. From this day forward, the packs will not follow because of rank... but because of choice. And together, we will build something better."

There was a pause... and then the first howl rose. A sound of agreement. Of kinship. It spread through the clearing like fire through dry grass. One by one, wolves lifted their heads to the sky.

And Selina let Ama sing.

****

That evening, she returned to the glade... The one place untouched by war. The air there was different, softer. It smelled of wildflowers and pine, damp earth and peace. The sounds of the forest whispered through the leaves like a lullaby. Crickets chirping, a night bird calling in the distance, a gentle breeze rustling through branches that hadn't known fire.

 In the center of the glade, beneath the rising moon, she laid the carved stone bearing her twin brother's crescent mark into the earth. As her fingers brushed the cool surface of the stone, a memory rose... given to her by the Goddess... of his laugh echoing through the trees as a boy, his hair catching sunlight like spun gold. Then the voice of the Goddess cryptically whispered in her mind, *"He is happy across the Veil in play with your Mother. He will be reborn again soon and you will be reunited... just in a different role."*

She whispered to Ama, *"Do you know what she meant?"*

Ama, with a wolfish grin lay down, curling up at the back of Selina's mind, refusing to say a word.

The burial was silent. She knelt in the soft grass, fingertips trailing the soil as if to hold his memory there. Luke stood beside her, a quiet pillar of strength. Galen flanked her other side.

She didn't speak at first. The wind carried enough words.

But her breath hitched once, twice, before she whispered, "I will carry you. Always."

And as if answering her, the moonlight deepened casting a silvery glow across the glade like a benediction. In the center under the light of the rising moon, she laid the carved stone bearing her twin brother's crescent mark into the earth.

****

Later that night, the clearing glowed with silver fireflies and moon-glass flowers blooming along the edges of the trees. The twins waited for her there.

She found them beside the small brook, where light rippled over their hands, casting reflections like threads of silver across their skin. The air was cool and fragrant with moss and water lilies. Nathaniel's fingers brushed the surface, sending tiny ripples dancing toward the far bank, while Xavier ran his hand through the damp grass, grounding himself.

Nathaniel was the first to speak, his voice low and reverent. "You don't have to say anything."

Selina moved closer, her steps slow but sure. "But I will," she said and her voice trembled with the weight of choice. "You stood beside me. And I know now... fate didn't choose for me. I did."

Xavier stepped forward, his eyes searching hers. "Does that mean... we...?"

She reached for them both, her hands finding theirs. Her forehead pressed against Nathaniel's chest, then to Xavier's shoulder. The scent of their skin... familiar, grounding... wrapped around her like home.

Her voice was soft as she replied, "It means we start walking forward. Together."

****

The moon reached its peak, casting silvery beams across the ancient glade like the breath of the goddess herself. Mist rose from the moss-covered ground, curling through tree roots and drifting over stone, as if the earth were exhaling the final weight of war. The air smelled of pine resin and ash, old magic and new beginnings... A mingling of past and future.

The packs gathered slowly at first, emerging from the shadows of the trees and the edges of the clearing. Some limped from wounds from rogue attacks in their territories; others bore freshly scrubbed armor and worn cloaks. Wolves padded silently between their human forms, nuzzling their kin. Elders leaned on carved staffs, younglings clung to parents' hands. There were wary glances, hesitant nods—but there were also tears, and cautious smiles.

Faces from every territory—Frostedge, Ironfang, Greenfen, and more—turned toward the center of the glade. Some bore bruises and scars from the final battle. Others still wore bandages and smelled of poultices. Yet all stood shoulder to shoulder, a tapestry of survival woven in flesh and fur.

Not to kneel... But to stand. To join.

Selina stood at their center, her wolf blazing inside her, her heart no longer torn by prophecy, but tempered by it.

Ama howled.

And the forest answered.

Under the light of the moon, amid the wolves and warriors, the age of unity was born. And this time...

It would not break.

Chapter 27 – Epilogue – New Moon

Several months had passed since the battle beneath the Hollow Veil, but the land was still healing... not just in soil and stone, but in spirit. Across the territories, word had spread: the prophecy had been fulfilled not through conquest, but through unity. The Moon-Blessed Alpha had risen, and the old ways had been broken.

The land wasn't the only thing that healed with the passage of time... Selina had accepted the twins as her mates, and together they grown. Not only in strength, but in a love that felt destined. Forged through trials. Strengthened by trust. Their bond stronger than any that had come before...

Selina walked slowly through the glade, now just a short journey from their pack since the evil had been purged. It bloomed again with new life. The trees stood taller, their limbs full of green and gold. Wildflowers covered the earth like woven tapestries, and the stream that once whispered through the clearing now sang. It was early morning, and dew still clung to the leaves like blessings left behind by the stars. Birds sang low and sweet. Peace, for once, had taken root.

She paused beside the stone she had laid for her twin brother. Moss had crept around its base, but the crescent carving still shone in the morning light. She knelt beside it, running her fingers over the surface, and smiled.

"You're still with me," she whispered.

A breeze stirred the branches overhead, and Ama murmured in her mind: *"He is closer than you know. His soul never left. Only waited."*

Selina rose and continued down the path.

At the edge of the glade, her twins waited. Xavier held a woven wrap against his chest, where a newborn stirred, barely more than a breath of warmth wrapped in linen and soft wool. The child cooed once, then yawned, revealing the smallest crescent-shaped birthmark glowing faintly above his heart.

Selina approached, her breath caught, awe blooming across her face as she reached out. Time seemed to still as she looked as the faint crescent mark over his heart shimmered faintly… Like moonlight catching on water, as Selina's fingers brushed his cheek, her hand trembled. His hair… his hair catching sunlight like spun gold. She saw not just a child, but a soul she had once known… a soul she had mourned, returned in new form… one achingly familiar.

"He has your eyes and your mark," Nathaniel said quietly.

Xavier leaned in with a soft chuckle. "He stills whenever you're near… almost like he remembers you."

Her throat tightened. The whisper of the goddess came back to her: *He will be reborn again soon… just in a different role.*

Selina bent low and pressed a kiss to the baby's brow. "Welcome back," she murmured.

The moon that night rose new and silver, casting its gentle light across the newly built council circle. No thrones, no altars… just a ring of stone benches and standing torches, and voices raised not in command but in collaboration. Representatives of the major packs spoke side by side. Disagreements flared, but were met with laughter, not war cries. New treaties were written by shared hand, not dictated by rank—etched into stone not as laws, but as living promises to the future.

As Selina watched, Ama lay curled deep in her spirit, restful and at peace.

The child slept nestled between Nathaniel and Xavier beneath the stars, as wolves howled not in mourning... but in celebration.

And high above them, the moon, new, watchful, whole... cradled the sky like a promise kept. And beneath its light, a future finally free to bloom.

Once marked, once lost. Now chosen, now whole.

About the Author

From the shadows of a broken childhood marked by poverty and trauma, Amaterina carved a path with grit, heart, and resilience, ultimately forging a meaningful career as a Registered Nurse and devoting more than two decades to caring for others. Yet even amidst the demands of healthcare, the quiet voice never faded... a persistent whisper by her muse, tugging at her soul with stories begging to be told. When life brought her to a pivotal crossroads, she embraced her creative calling and completed her debut book in just one week.

A fierce protector of those she holds dear, Amaterina is loyal to the core and generous to a fault with anyone fortunate enough to be part of her inner circle. She loves deeply, protects fiercely, and never stops asking questions, driven by an endless curiosity.

When she's not writing or caring for patients, she explores the world through books, photography, and deep conversation. Her life is filled with impromptu photo shoots of anything that sparks wonder, and the kind of laughter that only grows in the company of those she trusts and cares for deeply. She's a lifelong rescuer—not only of animals and patients, but of moments, memories, and meaning...offering sanctuary wherever she can.

Titles by Amaterina:

Altering Her World to Save His Sanity

Sensual Seductions – A Collection of Erotic Stories

Silver Blood, Shadowed Sky

A Dragon's Love

Altering Her World to Save His Sanity

By Amaterina

He was drowning in silence.
She became the quiet that saved him.

Shannon doesn't believe in fairytales. A trauma nurse with her own scars, she's learned to survive by keeping her world orderly, her heart guarded, and her past buried. But when a late-night swipe on a dating app connects her to a man named Jack — guarded, enigmatic, and emotionally frayed — everything begins to shift.

Jack isn't looking for love. Haunted by his past and tormented by PTSD, he's spent years avoiding anything that feels like connection. But Shannon offers something he's never known: patience without pressure, kindness without pity, and a presence steady enough to silence the noise inside his head.

What begins as cautious friendship slowly grows into something tender, something true — a sanctuary built one fragile moment at a time. But healing isn't linear, and when the ghosts of Jack's past collide with the weight of Shannon's sacrifices, they'll both have to decide: how far will they bend for love... and what are they willing to change to protect it?

A poignant, slow-burn romance about trauma, trust, and the quiet strength of choosing someone—every single day.

 Amazon Customer

★★★★★ **The most heartfelt book I've ever read**

Reviewed in the United States on July 14, 2025

What I loved most about this book was how personal it felt. It was gentle, deeply empathetic, charming and very sweet. It's two people at different points in their emotional healing journeys, with her farther along, showing him the way. I want so much more like this!

Sensual Seductions

A Collection of Erotic Stories

By Amaterina

Dive into a world where desire simmers behind office doors, tension crackles in snowbound cabins, and pleasure drips from every whispered word and forbidden glance. In this collection of scorching tales, Amaterina delivers stories that are as emotionally charged as they are wildly erotic.

- In **Office Secrets**, a high-stakes flirtation explodes into a torrid power exchange between coworkers who can't keep their hands—or rules—off each other.

- **Snowbound** strands one woman in a remote lodge with three irresistible men, where icy weather leads to blazing-hot connections and sensual indulgence.

- In **The Demon in the Mirror**, a burned-out woman on a soul-searching retreat finds herself entangled with a seductive, supernatural presence that awakens something primal and unrelenting within her.

Each story is laced with intensity, consent-driven kink, emotional evolution, and a slow burn that bursts into full-bodied heat.

Whether it's dominance and submission, group chemistry, or otherworldly passion, *Sensual Seductions* offers a decadent escape for readers craving more than just a one-night fantasy.

Surrender to the temptation. Your desires are waiting.

A Dragon's Love

A Tale of Curse and Courage

By Amaterina

Bound by a goddess's wrath, Fafnir—the once-proud prince—has spent centuries imprisoned in the body of a dragon, cursed to live in isolation and darkness. Every hundred years, a village offers a sacrifice to appease the mysterious beast in the cave... but none have ever returned.

Until Bethina.

Chosen by fate and betrayed by tradition, Bethina is sent to what should have been her death. But instead of a monster, she finds a soul as lonely and burdened as her own. Fafnir offers her a bargain: companionship in exchange for her life. But what begins as survival blossoms into something far deeper and more dangerous—hope, desire, and the whisper of love.

As secrets unravel and old wounds resurface, Bethina must decide if she can love the beast... and if that love is powerful enough to break the curse before time runs out.

Lush, romantic, and enchantingly dark, *A Dragon's Love* is a tale of sacrifice, resilience, and the transformative magic of the heart.

Silver Blood, Shadowed Sky
By Amaterina

They called her wolfless. They called her ghost. But the moon never forgets its chosen.

In a world ruled by ancient prophecy and ruthless packs, Selina is born before her time—marked by the goddess, bound to a secret wolf spirit, and cast out by those who should have protected her. Branded an outcast and hidden in plain sight, she survives years of cruelty, silence, and betrayal with nothing but her will—and a wolf named Amaris stirring within.

But fate doesn't forget.

As the eclipse nears and the Hollow Veil rises, Selina's hidden power begins to awaken. She is no longer just the broken girl at the edge of the pack—she is the prophecy incarnate. The Moon-Blessed Alpha. And she's not alone.

Now, hunted by shadowed priests and stalked by a rogue bound in madness, Selina must gather allies, face the sins of the past, and claim her place before the darkness consumes the realm.

Because the moon is rising.

And this time, she howls back.

A powerful fantasy of survival, sisterhood, betrayal, and becoming—perfect for readers who love fierce heroines, forbidden bonds, and epic prophecy.

www.ingramcontent.com/pod-product-compliance
Lightning Source LLC
Chambersburg PA
CBHW060147130626
46556CB00006B/2533